Awake at Dusk

Awake at Dusk

KRISTY L. BREWER

Copyright © 2014 by Kristy L. Brewer.

Library of Congress Control Number:		2014919966
ISBN:	Hardcover	978-1-5035-1429-4
	Softcover	978-1-5035-1431-7
	eBook	978-1-5035-1430-0

All rights reserved. No part of this book may be reproduced or transmitted in any form or by any means, electronic or mechanical, including photocopying, recording, or by any information storage and retrieval system, without permission in writing from the copyright owner.

This is a work of fiction. Names, characters, places and incidents either are the product of the author's imagination or are used fictitiously, and any resemblance to any actual persons, living or dead, events, or locales is entirely coincidental.

Any people depicted in stock imagery provided by Thinkstock are models, and such images are being used for illustrative purposes only.
Certain stock imagery © Thinkstock.

This book was printed in the United States of America.

Rev. date: 01/27/2015

To order additional copies of this book, contact:
Xlibris
1-888-795-4274
www.Xlibris.com
Orders@Xlibris.com

To my husband Jessie
To our wonderful children
To my mom Dollie
To all my Family and Friends who supported me
To Eric, Bertha, & April
Who walk No more but are carried in my heart
Thank You

Preface

What do you do when you find yourself lying awake, staring at the ceiling night after night? I ask because for years this was my reality; I found no rest in sleep. I was constantly jerked awake, drenched in sweat and trembling in fear. I remember searching frantically around me, struggling to grasp hold of my pillow and blanket, fearing that I may drift back into the troubling depths of the unknown.

I can't say that the jokes from family and friends when I tried to explain the images that haunted me while I slept were unexpected. I went to my pastor, who was also my father. He told me to stop eating before going to bed. I sought out prophets and dream interpreters, but the interpretations I received seemed to be parallel to my life and current events. I couldn't help thinking that the dreams, many reoccurring, held a deeper meaning. I started writing in my journal, which I named the Dream Catcher, and as the years passed, the images from my dreams began to manifest as my reality. They became a road map that pieced together like a puzzle inadvertently revealing my destiny.

The narrative and characters in this story are fictional, but the dreams are real.

Prologue

The Future

Heather looked around her living room, furiously searching for anything to throw at him as he stood there with his back to her, refusing to acknowledge her presence.

"Are you listening!" she yelled. The pressure of blood pumping in her temple increased as anger clouded her thoughts.

In total disgust, she turned and ran into the kitchen. Her eyes darted from the sink to the cabinets as she snatched the drawers open and slammed them shut loudly, not sure what she was searching for. Her hands settled on the assortment of knives on the counter. She grabbed the largest knife from the set and ran back into the living room.

With all her strength, she grabbed his arm, trying to force him to turn to her, but he ignored her attempts.

"Look at me!" she screamed, waving the knife in his face, thinking it would scare him, but his expression never changed.

After a moment, she realized how foolish she must look to him. It was then that she felt an overwhelming sense of exhaustion. The weight that she was carrying was too heavy, and her knees buckled under the pressure.

"I can't do this," she whispered from her knees. "Baby, I'm tired."

Heather looked up, fighting the tears that she felt at the back of her throat. "Don't you love me?" Her hurt and pain was undisguised.

He didn't answer. He continued to look away; his mind was on something else.

"It's like that . . . I'm nothing to you?" she said matter-of-factly, looking at the knife in her hand.

Rubbing the tip of the knife against her chest, a moment passed as she thought about it . . . a permanent end.

What if I did it? Would it even matter? She was disgusted with herself for her thoughts.

"You're not worth it." She sneered through clenched teeth as she stumbled to her feet. Immediately a sharp pain shot through her body as she gasped for breath. The wooden knife was covered in blood emerging from a gaping wound between her breasts. In confusion, Heather stumbled into the kitchen, trying to understand how and what happened. She grabbed the side of the table in an effort to steady her balance. She could feel her heart beating in her temple as the blood began to cover her hands and pour onto the table. The room was spinning around her, and she fell to the floor.

"What have I done?" she said to herself, looking at her hands and feeling the thick blood that now covered her.

She began calling his name.

Minutes passed.

Her eyes began to roll as she felt herself fading away.

Opening her eyes slightly, she saw him standing in the doorway.

"Help me!" Despair was evident in her voice.

He walked toward her. Through her tears, she saw him stand over her, expressionless, as he looked down at her.

"I'm dying!" she cried, reaching for him.

He slowly backed away. His empty eyes met hers as he left the kitchen.

"Please . . . call someone . . .," she pleaded.

His response was only to close the door quietly behind him.

Heather's heart was beating frantically. She mustered all her strength and slid across the floor to the back door.

So many thoughts in her head, but she could not panic. Refusing to focus on the amount of blood leaving a wide smear behind her, she managed to crawl through the back door.

She lifted her eyes to the most unexpected sight: before her were two glass doors that read Emergency Entrance.

In deep wonderment, she inched forward, causing the doors to slide open. A flood of people exited the hospital, each walking quickly in her direction. Not one of them noticed Heather's sprawling figure on the floor; one by one, they stepped over her. Heather looked at the long hall in front of her. The white walls, glossy white floors, and florescent lights from the ceiling created a glare, and she lowered her tired eyes. She didn't want to move forward because the blood would stain the floors.

She looked at the shoes as they stepped over her. Feeling empty and defeated, she mustered enough strength to grab one of them as it moved past her. "Can you help me?" Her voice was barely a whisper.

A man looked down at her, totally surprised that she was there. He saw the puddle of blood that surrounded her and immediately yelled for help. Several people ran to assist him as he lifted her off the floor and onto a tall metal table. Heather sighed in relief, knowing that someone was finally going to help her. She closed her eyes to block out the bright white lights, but she could hear people talking over her head.

Only a few minutes passed when she felt a hand press her shoulder and a low voice in her ear. "Ma'am, you're free to go."

Heather's eyes shot open. "What!"

Immediately she began groping her chest, searching for the gaping hole, but it was no longer there.

"What did you do?"

Her mind was racing as she watched the doctor remove the gloves from his hands. He placed his hands behind her and assisted her as she sat up clumsily.

He patted her back, comforting her. "Everything is fine now. You lost a lot of blood during the miscarriage, but you'll be fine." His sympathetic glance and gentle hand helped her dismount from the tall table and guided her to the exit.

"A miscarriage?" she repeated with mixed emotions. The thought that she had unknowingly carried a life inside her was overwhelming. Heather was overcome with confused relief as she walked through the sliding doors of the hospital and immediately found herself standing at her front door. She stood there for a moment, staring at the wooden door that towered over her, making her feel small and vulnerable. Anxiety replaced all emotions as she reached out to turn the doorknob.

There he was, sitting in the recliner with his head resting in his hands. He appeared to be meditating as she rushed into the house, anxious to tell him of the strange turn of events.

She reached for him.

"I'm okay." She smiled.

"I went to the hospital, and I'm okay." As her hand touched his shoulder, he looked up, and his eyes caught hers with a piercing stare that stopped her.

"What's wrong?" she began backing away from him.

His lips curled, and deep lines creased his forehead.

Her hands were shaking as fear overtook her as he looked at her with disgust.

"Why aren't you dead?" he spoke quietly.

Heather stepped away from him as he rose from the chair.

"You are supposed to be dead!" A husky, unfamiliar voice came out of his parted lips.

~

Heather's eyes burned from sweat and tears as she forced herself to wake. Her heart was racing as she stepped from the tub. Trembling hands grabbed a towel, and she quickly rushed through each room in her quaint apartment, making sure all the windows were locked. Her paranoia not satisfied with knowing that it was only a dream.

She started to feel better as she approached her son's room where Buzz Lightyear greeted her at the door. Since turning three, Harley only wanted Buzz. From curtains and pillows to pajamas, undies, and socks, Buzz it was. Heather pretended she was tired of the Buzz obsession, but she loved every bit of it. Just thinking of how he kicked and screamed in the store until she bought the huge Buzz poster made her smile.

She watched as Harley smiled in his sleep, playing with angels, she assumed.

How precious he is . . . so innocent, she thought to herself. *He has no worries, no pain, no fear, and no haunting dreams.*

Careful not to wake him, she leaned over to kiss him.

The nagging pain in her temples forced her to leave her son's peaceful sanctuary and head to the medicine cabinet. There were times that she dreaded taking the assortment of pills, but it took four years and seeing the effect of not taking them to change her mind. She swallowed the pills that have now become her only way to escape the troubling dreams.

Heather Ford

The Past and Present

Chapter One

~The Past~

Heather Ford stood at the back of the small auditorium, watching the girls as they finished rehearsals for the upcoming holiday performance. She walked down the aisle, motioning for the last person to get in place on the stage.

Heather was the drama teacher of Fellowship Academy, the only all-girls school in Pontiac, Michigan. She enjoyed working with the girls. Many of them started the year off shy and gained confidence as the year progressed.

She glanced at her watch. She could see from the small windows that the sun had gone down and thanks to daylight savings, it seemed to be much later than the six o'clock hour. Heather clapped loudly and motioned for all the girls to gather around her as Rita finished her poetic expression, but an unexpected applause caused her to turn her attention to the far corner at the back of the auditorium.

"Outstanding!" Chavell Goodman's voice echoed through the auditorium as he walked down the aisle toward her.

Heather was surprised to see him; it wasn't often that Sister Nena would allow visitors from other schools on the campus, and Saint Paul Academy, a school for distinguished gentlemen, was definitely no exception.

"Mr. Goodman, how are you?" Heather's smile was genuine as she shook his hand and greeted the three young men he had in tow.

She could feel the reserved stared from the girls as they gathered on the stage… whispering in wonderment about the visitors.

"Take five, girls."

"This will only take a moment," he began. "Sister Nena told me to bring the boys by so that you could meet them and decide how you wanted to use them into the Christmas Eve program. I would like to introduce Jayden, Marcos, and Antonio." The young boys stepped forward as he called their names.

Heather masked her confusion and smiled at each of the young boys. They each appeared to be in their early teens. Jayden smiled effortlessly and stepped forward to shake her hand, and Marcos quickly followed suit. Antonio was much more reserved, smiling briefly and staying near Mr. Goodman's side.

"Mr. Goodman, I think you may have misunderstood Sister Nena. I think she meant the fine arts department. Theater arts is not scheduled to perform in the Christmas program," Heather said while guiding them to the door.

"Oh, Mr. Goodman, you made it . . ."

Heather was startled as Sister Nena sauntered happily toward them.

"And these must be the young gentlemen." Sister Nena embraced each of the boys. "Oh, we are looking forward to the community Christmas Eve program, aren't we, Ms. Ford?"

Heather tried her best to erase the dumbfounded expression from her face but failed drastically.

"Sister Nena, can I have a moment with you?"

The sister continued her exaggerated enthusiasm for the boys and pretended not to hear Heather speaking.

"Mr. Goodman, can you excuse us for a moment?" Heather regretted the look on Mr. Goodman's face as she addressed him directly, but Sister Nena knew that her calendar was booked, and Christmas Eve of all days was out of the question.

"Sure, sure . . . there is obviously some confusion. Ms. Ford, if you would like us to come back another—"

"No need for that, Mr. Goodman," Sister Nena cut him off immediately and dismissed Heather with one wave of her hand.

"It's an honor for the mayor to ask our schools to join this event. And these young men . . ." She walked over, staring at each of them. "Ms. Ford, these young men are being vetted for admission to the Boys Academy next fall. You do understand that there is a waiting list an arm-length long, but these boys have been given an opportunity that many haven't."

Nodding reassuringly at Mr. Goodman, she turned sharply to Heather.

"They have been identified as youths that can overcome their troubling beginning and become great achievers and examples in their community. But they first must demonstrate leadership, discipline, and complete community service as a part of their admission requirement."

Heather listened as Sister Nena put on the performance of her life in front of Mr. Goodman.

Mr. Goodman shifted his weight from foot to foot uncomfortably. He could barely contain himself. "Ms. Ford, I do apologize. I was not aware that you had not agreed to this."

Heather eyes moved from Mr. Goodman's obvious embarrassment to the young boys who seemed to be aware of the thick tension between them, and she managed a reassuring smile.

"An important part of being a professional is to expect the unexpected," Sister Nena cut into her thoughts. "No need to apologize, Mr. Goodman, your school does not have a fine arts program and we do." Her tone sharpened. "So naturally, if we want to help the community with this kind of program, then we have to work together, and I am sure Ms. Ford understands this."

Sister Nena who was now looking more like the witch from the Wizard of Oz was insufferable, but Heather knew that there was no end in arguing with her. From that moment on, she smiled and nodded, agreeing to everything that was said without listening to any of it.

~

The weeks leading up to Harvest production were grueling. Heather decided against changing the summer production but added a few new acts for the girls so she could dedicate as much time as possible to the boys. The boys worked as stagehands most days and proved to be a good asset to the theater department. One of the skits required a table, a lamp, and a floor rug. Heather, grateful for the extra hands, took the boys to her house, and within an hour, the stage was set. Heather tried to work on their parts after the girls finished practicing since their performance wasn't until Christmas. It took Antonio a minute to adjust to being onstage, especially with all the girls in the audience looking on, but Jayden and Marcos proved to be ideal. They loved the attention. Jayden especially. He charmed all the girls with jokes and side glances, causing them to giggle whenever he took the stage.

Chapter Two
· · · · · · · · · · · · · · · · · ·

Heather watched her lead student as she walked across the stage and gracefully lowered herself to the floor while waving a black silk scarf around her head. Heather smiled inwardly, knowing how timid Rita was, and now here she was, performing "In the Shadow" all by herself.

"Are you any different from me?"

Rita's voice echoed through the empty auditorium as she began the rendition that Heather wrote for her the previous year. "I need more volume!" Heather yelled from the floor. The acoustics in the auditorium was horrible, and after a year of requesting cordless mikes, Heather was beginning to accept the fact that they would probably not get them. Feeling a sense of urgency, her mind wandered as she thought about the growing to-do list.

*"I know everything about you.
I follow you everywhere you go."*

The emotion in Rita's voice drew Heather's attention to the stage. Rita jumped to her feet and ran from one side of the stage to the other as she poured her emotion into the skit.

"Okay, that's good." Heather nodded as Rita's voice projected louder.

Rita spoke to the empty chairs as if they were full of people. She moved her body as if dancing in her partner's embrace. She was presenting herself as if she were her own shadow, arguing the significance of her existence. Heather watched Rita embrace the poem with all five of her senses. She was proud of her, knowing that this particular skit was very difficult to pull off, and Rita's performance was flawless.

Heather turned her attention to the girls. "Okay, listen up, girls. We have one more rehearsal before the Thanksgiving program." Heather paused as the girls gathered around her, moaning and complaining. "I'm going to give you a week off before we start working with the boys . . . for the Christmas Eve productions." The moaning got louder. She knew that they were not happy about adding the Christmas Eve event to the schedule and were not enthused about the boys practicing and performing with them.

"Girls?" Heather waited for the girls to get quiet. "We've had a tough schedule, but remember that you were chosen to perform at the community Christmas bash this year because you're the best, and I want you to know that I'm proud of you." Heather looked at the smiles that were slowly spreading across the girls' faces as they embraced and headed outside into the crisp fall winds.

~

Heather braced herself against the wind as she ran through the parking lot to her car. She started the engine and glanced at the gas hand, thankful that she didn't have to stop for gas. The school wasn't far from her house, and within thirty minutes, she was unlocking her front door, tripping out of her shoes, and jumping in the shower.

She had an hour and a half to get to her girlfriend's thirtieth birthday party, and she couldn't find anything to wear. Her room was completely cluttered with clothes, shoes, and everything imaginable left from her weekly routine of work, home, and sleep. She rarely had time to do anything else, but tonight was going to be an exception.

Heather was eager to break free of her routine and have some adult conversation for a change. She put on her famous black-and-white bodysuit, knowing that it complimented her figure. She never wore heavy makeup. She touched up her eyebrows with her razor, applied mascara, and touched her lips with color. She looked in the mirror and liked what she saw—a tired black beauty, but no one would know unless she told them.

Heather sped up on the highway, quickly putting distance between her and her house. Thankful for the light traffic, Heather was able to relax and enjoy the twenty-minute drive through the country roads. She reached in the console for her cell phone and realized she left it charging in the bathroom. "Dang!" she said loudly and instead turned the radio on.

She could feel the weight of the day resting heavily on her shoulders. She couldn't believe Sister Nena had scheduled this last-minute event on Christmas Eve and had volunteered her to train male students to perform on an all-girls drama team without notifying her. Just thinking about it made her blood boil.

~

The music was deafening, and the club was packed. Heather saw that her girls were already there and that the table was filling up with bottles of a wide variety of liquor from men trying to get noticed. Heather smiled to herself, knowing that none of her friends were heavy drinkers. *This will be interesting*, she thought.

"Happy birthday, Cheri!" Heather yelled over the noise as she embraced her good friend. "Are you better?" Heather asked, sincerely concerned about Cheri. She had been having panic attacks all week, stressing about turning thirty.

"Girl, I'm good!" Cheri yelled over the crowd, turning her back to her friend to show off her shape and being careful not to waste her wine. "Look at this body, this ain't no thirty-year-old body." She laughed. "These chicks ain't got nothing on this."

Heather laughed as Cheri pointed directly at a group of young girls making their way to the dance floor.

"Tonight's *my* night, and I want everyone to dance and have a good time. Here, drink up." She put her glass to Heather's lips. "You're not sitting down on me tonight—relax!"

Heather took the glass from Cheri and gulped it down quickly. She knew if she poured a glass of anything, she would never drink it. She looked around the table, wondering how Cheri managed to book the VIP section. Cheri had decorated the tables with white cloth and silver and sparkling glass accents that gave it an elegant feel. Looking at the women standing around the table, she could see that all of them had stepped their game up. This was the most beautiful corner in the club, and it seemed as if every guy knew it.

"Hey, sweetie." Heather sat down next to their mutual friend, Janet. She was startled as she hugged her and saw that she had on gray contacts. Janet laughed when she saw her reaction.

"You like 'em?" Janet blinked her eyes seductively.

"I love them, so tigress and sexy," Heather said, laughing with her friend.

It had been a long time since she and her friends got out, and just to see everyone enjoying themselves made her enjoy the moment that much more.

The table was soon swarmed by guys looking for conversations with benefits. Heather and Janet did everything possible to avoid eye contact with any of them, but the swarm was soon becoming unnerving. She and Janet watched as Cheri and the other girls fulfilled their promise to dance the night away. It wasn't long before Heather grew tired of getting bumped and pushed by the swollen crowd. The constant unwanted advances from the men finally forced them to take refuge in the ladies' room.

"I think I'm going to head home," Heather told Janet as they stood in line, waiting for a stall. Running away from the annoying group of drunk men that had set up camp around their table was the last straw for Heather. "What time is it?" she asked.

Janet glanced at her watch. "It's almost two. They're going to turn the lights on in a minute anyway."

They entered the smoke-filled room, Janet motioning at all the people loitering and impeding their progress.

"We need to get Cheri and go before we get caught in this traffic."

As they inched their way through the crowded room, Heather felt someone grab her arm. All night she had been fighting off men, and now that the exit was within her reach, she had to give her famous "don't dance, no phone, not interested" speech.

Heather turned and was surprised to find herself face-to-face with a very handsome man.

Chapter Three

Omar Eden just took a chance. He saw that she and her friend had turned down every guy that came to the table. He had sent over a bottle of wine and had the waitress put it in her hand and point in his direction, but she didn't even turn around to see who sent it. He watched her all night, but she never looked his way, and here she was, right in front of him. She had been with her friend all night, and he could see that she was trying to stay close to her. He thought if he separated them, he would have a better chance at having a conversation. The surprised look on her face when he grabbed her was not anger but irritation. He quickly decided to take her a step farther. He didn't waste time thinking as he slowly pulled her through the crowd and onto the dance floor.

"Excuse me!" She was looking at him no longer in irritation but in anger.

"What's your name?" Omar decided to ignore her anger. He watched her all night and didn't think she would make a scene. He started dancing and somehow knew she would eventually start dancing too.

He noticed as he got into the groove of the music that she was staring blankly at him, so he decided on a new approach. He placed two figures in his mouth and whistled loudly, getting the DJ's attention. "Slow it down," he mouthed, knowing the DJ would read his lips, and immediately, the music changed to a slow jam as he requested.

"Why didn't you drink the wine that I had sent to your table?" Omar took a step forward and placed one hand on her waist. He moved from side to side, and just as he thought, she began to move as well. *Making progress*, he thought to himself.

"So what's your name?" he whispered in her ear as he let the music work its magic, proudly showing off his moves.

Heather couldn't believe the nerve of this guy. The only reason she didn't walk off the dance floor was because there was something different about him. He didn't seem to be like the drunks she spent most of the night running from. He was dressed really sharp in a collarless buttoned-down shirt, nice slacks, nice shoes, and minimal jewelry—very classy. He was older but very clean-cut and handsome; he also seemed to have some clout in the club. Heather had to admit he was quite impressive.

"I'm Heather, and you are?" *I may as well be nice, it's only a dance*, she thought.

"Everyone calls me Maury."

Heather noticed the crowd on the dance floor moved back, allowing him to have the floor as he danced in circles around her. She was impressed.

The lights came on abruptly as the song ended, and Heather smiled graciously, turning and walking away before he could ask for her number. She rushed as fast as the slow-moving crowd would allow and was relieved to find Janet and Cheri standing, waiting on her near the exit.

"Who was that guy?" Cheri said as soon as Heather got within earshot.

"He said his name is Mary or Mah'ree or something . . . Let's go," Heather replied, halfheartedly deciding to end the conversation before it began. "Are you riding back with me?" She smoothly turned the conversation to Cheri's inability to drive.

"No, she picked me up. I'm going to drive her car back and crash at her place." Janet got the keys from Cheri.

"Yeah." Cheri stumbled out the door. "She's my designated driver." Cheri's voice slurred noticeably as they said good-bye.

Heather welcomed the cold fresh air as she exited the club and crossed the parking lot to her car.

~

Janet pulled from the parking lot into the dense crowd of people exiting the club.

"Isn't that the guy Heather was dancing with?" Cheri asked, looking out the window.

Janet looked at the group of guys crossing the street right in front of the car. "Yep, and he's a cutie."

"Blow!" Cheri yelled, not giving Janet a chance to react as she pressed the horn.

Omar immediately turned at the sound of the horn. The bright headlights blurred his vision, but he knew it had to be a female blowing at him, so he walked blindly to the window with a big smile on his face.

"Hey, where's your friend?" He recognized Janet immediately. He leaned his head into the car, looking in the backseat.

"You mean Heather?" Janet said with a malicious smile creeping on her face. "She's in that car right behind us."

Both Janet and Cheri watched as Omar walked to Heather's car.

~

Heather's brain was screaming all kinds of obscenities at Janet and Cheri when she saw them send that guy back to her car. A bit flustered, she slapped on a smile and reluctantly rolled the window down.

"Hey, beautiful," his voice came through the window with the cold air. Heather no longer welcomed the brisk cold air, and her mind was working overtime trying to think of how to get rid of him.

"Hi." She smiled, looking through her purse for her phone so that she could pretend to put his number in it. It didn't take long for her to remember where her phone was not. She sighed deeply and threw the purse onto the backseat.

"You were going to leave without saying good-bye, Ms. Hea-ther?" He pronounced her name completely, knowing by her expression that she was surprised he remembered it. "You know I want to call you, so are you going to make me beg for your number?"

Heather looked at him for a moment. "You know what," she said with a smile, "I enjoyed your dance so much that I'm going to give you my number on one condition."

"What's that?" he asked.

"You tell me the name your mother gave you." Her smile was genuine.

"Well, since you are so beautiful, I will tell you what my mother named me." He smiled and whispered, "Omar . . . Omar Eden."

"Okay, Mr. O-mar E-den," she pronounced his name as he had done hers and avoided eye contact by rummaging through the console, trying to find something to write on. She found a black pen and a faded receipt and wrote her number on the back.

He really does seem like a nice guy, she reassured herself as she handed her number out the window. She hardly ever gave her real number to strangers, but tonight, she smiled politely at the handsome stranger before rolling her window up.

Omar turned to see the black Infiniti inch its way through traffic. Stephon had gotten the car from the parking garage and was now disregarding every driving law, trying to bypass the heavy traffic. He smiled to himself, knowing the other drivers were probably pissed, and watched as Stephon crossed the grass and straddled the curb, stopping a few inches from Heather's back bumper.

Realizing he could go no farther, Stephon put the car in park and jumped out. "You like that . . . you like that?" Stephon yelled. "I'm wheeling it, baby!" Omar laughed as Stephon tossed him his keys. Seeing Omar leaving Heather's window, Stephon whispered and nodded toward her car. "You get that?"

Omar patted his front pocket where he had stuck the small piece of paper that Heather handed him. "Don't ever doubt a playa." He laughed, shaking Stephon's hand again.

Omar took a Black & Mild cigar from his pocket and cupped his hand to keep the flame from the lighter lit as he inhaled deeply. The brown paper burned and caught the flame as he felt the warmth cover the front of his face and travel down his throat and through his nose.

He took another cigar from his pocket and handed it to his best friend standing next to him. Stephon grabbed it, lit it quickly, and exhaled.

"That tire looks low," Stephon said through the thick smoke, gesturing at the back tire of the Heather's car.

"It's all right." Omar looked at the tire briefly and shrugged.

"What about you, did you get the digits?" he asked smugly, knowing Stephon hardly ever scored numbers when they were out together.

"Hell yeah, you doubting me?"

Stephon saw the traffic moving ahead and used that opportunity to head back to the car.

Omar looked at Stephon as he walked away.

"You lying . . . I know you lying." He laughed. "Prove it."

Omar could see Stephon's jaw tighten as he grinded the tip of the cigar between his teeth. Omar couldn't contain himself. "Man, you know you didn't get no digits." He laughed at Stephon's obvious discomfort.

Chapter Four

Heather looked in her rearview mirror and noticed the men looking at the side of her car. Seeing how close the cars were riding to each other, she prayed that she hadn't gotten sideswiped by another car. The traffic inched slowly forward, and she was relieved that Omar was busy talking so she didn't have to wave goodbye as she pulled off. She drove three blocks and saw the three-car fender bender that had caused the long wait. She blew the horn as Janet turned off and headed to Cheri's house. Settling deep in her seat, she mentally prepared for the drive ahead of her.

Her thoughts drifted to the upcoming weeks. Thanksgiving was just around the corner, and she couldn't seem to focus on anything other than the work. *The girls are ready*, she thought, *but is it good enough? Sister Nena has been riding her back every day. Nothing satisfies that woman*, she thought. She had added only a few changes to the program from the previous year because with all the performances, they didn't have a lot of time to make major changes. *I wonder if Nena will notice.*

Heather rubbed her eyes as tiredness embraced her body.

Suddenly, the steering wheel was yanked from her grip, and she lost control of the car.

Heather screamed as the rear of the vehicle turned to the left and whipped the body of the car. She grabbed the wheel and tried to turn it to her right, but to her horror, the car swerved to the right and then to the left, forcing the vehicle into an uncontrollable spin. Her heart pounded in her ears as she looked out her window, seeing in the darkness the lights from her car. As if in slow motion, she could see that she was spinning off the road.

She could hear the screams of the tires. She grabbed the steering wheel and pulled as hard as she could. She felt her calf muscles straining from the pressure of her foot as she pumped the breaks as hard as she could.

The wheels locked.

Heather braced herself as the insurmountable force from the back of the vehicle yanked the car off the road and into the darkness. The car stopped immediately as weeds, brush, and pure darkness wrapped around the vehicle, forcing it to stop near the bottom of the ravine.

Her hands were shaking uncontrollably. The sound of her heartbeat filled the silence.

Heather looked out the window into the pitch-black night. The car settled deep into the darkness. She could see smoke coming from the back tires. *in the dark?*

light? how?

"I can't believe it . . . a blowout!" She barely recognized her voice as it cut through the emptiness of the night. Saying a prayer of thanks, she grabbed the sun visor hanging precariously in front of her face and opened the mirror to look at her throbbing face. Her bottom lip was bleeding from an apparent bite mark, and a bruise was forming right above her eye. As she touched her face, the small light from the visor bounced off her swollen knuckles, and she could see the cracks in the window where she must have hit her hands.

~

Otto Tillman could not stop his hands from shaking. He felt the heat building up in his chest slowly wrapping around his body, and beads of sweat burned his eyes. It had been a couple of hours since he had a fix, and the pressure behind his eyes was unbearable. He knew if he didn't get something in his system, he was going to start throwing up until he passed out.

He needed money.

"Where is it, Mama?" He pushed past his mother as she blocked the way into her bedroom.

"Otto, baby, I told you I don't have it. I had to pay the utility bill yesterday." Gal knew he wasn't listening. She hated when her son got like this. She watched helplessly as Otto rummaged through her stuff. He pulled every drawer from the dresser and threw each one to the floor after he searched every inch of them. Opening her closet, he fell to his knees and went through every shoe and shoe box.

"Where is it?" Otto yelled.

Tears rolled from Gal's eyes as fear and sadness took over her. "I told you, baby, I don't have any money."

Four years have passed since he was discharged from the army. Soon after his arrival, she first started noticing alcohol abuse, then with prescription drugs, then cocaine. Right now, she wasn't sure what he's taking. He complained that he felt like his heart would explode if he didn't have his fix, and after watching him go through painful withdrawals, she tried to have money for him whenever he needed it.

"Otto, where are you going?" Gal yelled. Her voice trailed behind him as he slammed out the door. She hated when he left the house like this. Sometimes days or even weeks would pass before she would see him again.

There was nowhere for him to go. The small two-bedroom house sat in the middle of pasture a mile from the highway and a ten-minute drive to the town. She really thought moving this far from the city would stop him from leaving, but she was wrong.

Otto walked out of the house, slamming the door behind him. He knew she had hid the money somewhere. He walked into the darkness of the night toward the old shed that was tucked away in the tall grass at the back end of the property. His mind on the jar he found there a couple of weeks earlier that had eighty cents in it. Maybe he had overlooked something. He never noticed the falling temperature and that he didn't have on his coat.

Suddenly, a flicker of light caught his eye. He could tell it was coming from the direction of the highway, and the more he focused on the light, even in the distance he could tell that it wasn't moving. Otto's pace quickened as he trekked his way through the overgrown field toward the light.

~

Heather rested her head on the headrest. She was going to have to get the car towed, which means she was going to be without transportation next week. She pressed the OnStar emergency button on her rearview mirror and immediately heard a dial tone and then the welcoming sound of a woman's voice.

"OnStar, what's your emergency?"

Heather sat up quickly. "Um, hi, my name is Heather Ford, and I ran off the road. I had a flat, and I'm . . .," she could hear herself rambling.

"Okay, ma'am, just stay calm. I am checking your location. Are you hurt?" The operator's voice was very calming.

"My hands are bleeding, I haven't gotten out to check my legs yet." Heather rubbed her knees as she spoke.

"How many people are in the vehicle, and are there any other vehicles involved the accident?"

"No. I'm alone."

"Okay, Heather, I have dispatched the emergency vehicles to your location, and I will stay on the line until help arrives. By the way, my name is Tammy."

Heather was so thankful that she wasn't alone anymore. She leaned her head back and closed her eyes.

~

As he neared the car, he saw from the tracks that it had slid down the hill from the highway. He approached the rear of the car slowly, not sure what he would find. Rubbing his hand along the side of the car, he could see that the wheels were embedded deep into the soft ground. He looked through the back window and saw a lady in the front seat. He stood there a moment and saw that she wasn't moving, and as he edged closer, he saw the purse lying on the backseat.

He walked to the passenger window and saw change in the cup holder. He quietly pulled the handle, but the door was locked. He bent down on the ground, feeling for a brick big enough to shatter the window when he heard the driver door open.

~

The next ten minutes seemed like hours, and Heather felt pain shooting up her legs. Heather unzipped the zipper on her boots, knowing that she wouldn't be able to stand up in the two-inch heel. She opened her door and planted her feet securely on the ground, moving her toes and feet. She placed one hand on the door and the other on the seat as she stood up slowly.

The stiffness was in her right leg. Thinking it was because she had been sitting, she decided to take a few steps forward.

She took her first step, and when the pain shot up through her ankle and calf, she knew then that her leg was hurt pretty bad. She clumsily hobbled to get back into the car when she felt the presence of something behind her. She turned and saw a dark shadow hovering over her. Her scream muffled and shortened as the force of the massive blow to her head shook her entire body into darkness.

"Heather, are you there?" Tammy heard Heather's muffled scream and knew something was wrong.

"Heather, can you hear me?"

Tammy saw that the police vehicle was less than two minutes away. The ambulance was not far behind.

"I need officers and emergency medical service vehicle on Highway 51 northbound near County Road 375, all emergency vehicles needed possible 10-31 in progress." Tammy's voice echoed across the board.

Chapter Five

Ellis Saxton was at the end of his shift when the first call came through. The last emergency call was a heart attack, and if it hadn't been for his paramedic team, he knew the lady wouldn't have survived the transition to the hospital. "Dispatch, this is EMS #954 Ellis Saxton." Ellis spoke into the transmitter.

"What's your location, Ellis?" Tammy's board was lit up with calls coming in.

Ellis glanced briefly at the navigation system. "Southbound on Highway 51, about two miles from CR375."

"I have emergency vehicles already assigned to that emergency. You can stop and see if they need you because you're right on top of them, but I will need you to head back to town."

Ellis could see the emergency lights as he approached the scene. He wasn't sure what the emergency was but could see there were three police vehicles and one other ambulance on the scene. He took out his flashlight and navigated his way to the bottom of the ravine. It was obvious that the car had created the wide tracks as it slid down the ravine. Officers were walking around the vehicle, and some were walking in the field.

Ellis rushed over to the paramedic team as they attempted to turn the victim over. His training took over as he rushed to their side.

"What's the status?" he asked, looking at the amount of blood that had covered the victim's face.

"The victim is a female, nonresponsive, pulse very faint, laceration on hands and face, major blow to the back of the head, and serious amount of blood loss." The medics knew they had to stop the bleeding if the woman was going to make it. "We got it under control. We'll get her stabilized."

One of the medics nodded his appreciation to Ellis. "Can you get some identification for me?"

Ellis approached the officer taking pictures of the backseat. "Do we have the victim's ID, sir?"

"Yes, the vehicle is registered to a . . . Heather Ford." The officer looked at his notepad as he spoke. "We found the purse and wallet out there in the field. Her ID is going to be logged in as evidence for now."

Ellis looked at the officer in confusion. "Evidence?"

"Yeah, looks like the poor girl was robbed. The OnStar dispatcher was on the line with her when she was attacked. Pretty sad to think someone would do something like this." The officer shook his head in disgust. "We'll get 'em though. I got my boys going through that field right now, and the dogs will be out here in the morning. We'll get 'em."

Ellis ran up the hill toward the waiting paramedic. He knew that they wouldn't leave until they got her stable. Just seeing the ambulance sitting there crushed his heart, and he knew something was going wrong. He opened the back door to the van. "Her name is Heather, Heather Ford, and this is the result of a robbery."

"Okay, jump in . . . she's seizing. We need your hands." The driver grateful for Ellis's presence, jumped into the driver seat and radioed for a police escort and paged the emergency room. "Possible brain injury" The driver spoke quickly, reporting to the ER. "Four back-to-back seizures. Get ready! We will arrive in eleven minutes."

Ellis jumped into position, holding Heather on her side. Her body trembled uncontrollably. Her eyes rolling precariously at the violent nature of the seizure. He secured her head and watched as the other paramedic frantically worked to keep her stable. He prayed quietly as her body became still. This is the longest ride he ever had to ride.

Heather's body became tense again, and immediately, her eyes began to roll. Ellis struggled to secure the straps that were straining under the pressure of her flailing body.

"She's seizing! Her heart rate is dangerously low!" The other paramedic was yelling at the driver as she struggled to get the vitals, leaving Ellis to hold on as best he could. His heart ached, knowing there was nothing they could do.

~

The images in Heather's mind consumed her as calmness fell over her body like a blanket, and she slipped further from reality. *She found herself walking down a street alone in a neighborhood that seemed unfamiliar to her. She noticed the full green grass that was neatly cut in each yard and the line of fully developed trees casting a shadow along the sidewalk. As she walked, her eyes were scanning each of the yards when she noticed a big black dog watching her. The dog was standing under a tree but appeared to be tied up. Heather noticed the look in his eyes, and his gaze made her nervous. She had passed the dog and three houses as she sped up her pace. A weird feeling took over her as she felt her heart begin to race, and the hair on the back of her neck stood up. Something was wrong. She looked sharply over her shoulder, and the dog that was several houses back was now standing a few yards from her. She could see the whites of his eyes and the rise and fall of his chest as he took several deep breaths. As a warning to her, he revealed his teeth and rendered a grave snarl. Without further notice, he lunged toward her.*

Heather turned and ran as fast as she could. She could feel the heat from the big dog on her back. She ran on the porch and through the front door of a brick house. As she walked into the living room, it seemed familiar to her. She walked with her back to the wall, looking at the dog pacing back and forth on the porch. She looked out the window and saw the dog standing on its hind legs in front of the door. Then to her amazement, the dog turned the doorknob and pushed the door open. No longer a dog but a tall dark shadow of a man entered the house. Heather could hear only her screams as the man came closer to her.

"Get away from me!" She kicked at the man until he backed away.

She turned the corner and ran down the long narrow hallway. As she looked back, she could see that the dark figure was gone. She walked into the bedroom and saw a walk-in closet with a light on. Heather walked in the closet and immediately noticed that it was full of her clothes hanging in dry cleaners' plastic and her shoes neatly placed in shoe boxes that were stacked endlessly.

This is my house, she said to herself, but when did I move here? As she rubbed her hands along the clothes hanging, she saw that the closet was much deeper than she thought. She saw several unopened boxes and a beautiful bassinet tucked away in the corner, still wrapped in plastic. As she approached the crib, to her horror, she saw a newborn baby lying on the bed. The skin was a grayish color, its lips were chapped, and it lay lifeless.

Heather began ripping the plastic away from the baby's face. Her thoughts were running. Is this my baby? Where did she come from? As she picked up the baby, the delicate little mouth opened, and it took a deep breath. Color rushed into her cheeks, and she opened her eyes.

Heather fell to her knees, holding the baby tightly in her arms. How could I forget about you? Tears welled up as she kissed the baby's cheeks, each of her eyes, and her forehead. The baby looked at Heather intently, and her small hands brushed her face gently.

~

Heather opened her eyes, and the bright lights surprised her. She looked around the strange white room for her clothes, the stacks of shoes that lined the walls of her closet, and she looked down at her arms and saw that her baby was gone. Her heart jumped as fear overtook her. She tried to sit up, but the sharp pain in her head stopped her. She felt someone grabbing her and looked up and saw her mother standing there. She snatched her arms away.

"What did you do with her!" she yelled, trying to climb out of the bed. She began pulling the cover from the bed, trying to remove what felt like weights from her legs. Heather could feel the heat moving across her face as tears blinded her.

"Why are you doing this to me?" she cried as her hands grabbed at the nurse that was standing by her bed. "Where's my baby!" Heather looked at her mother who stood with her hands covering her face, weeping quietly. "Oh god!" Seeing her mother's tears, Heather's fear overtook her. "She's dead, isn't she?" Heather looked around the room at everyone as they stared blankly at her.

"Heather, you are in the hospital. You were in a very bad accident. You had major trauma to your head, but you're fine now. We are here to help you, and I'm going to take good care of you, okay." The nurse spoke calmly and motioned for Mrs. Ford to come forward.

"Your mother has been here all week." The nurse smiled reassuringly to Heather's mom while she slowly stroked the back of Heather's hand.

Heather looked around the room as if for the first time. *This is a hospital*, she thought.

"Did my baby make it?" she spoke quietly, grasping the nurse's hands tightly. The nurse looked at Heather, and her heart went out to her. Poor girl. She had been through so much, and now this. She took a deep breath as she felt the tears in her throat.

"There is no baby." The nurse saw the hurt in Heather's eyes as she turned away in denial.

"Heather," Mrs. Ford leaned forward, wiping the sweat and tears from her daughter's face, "you don't have any kids." Her mother's matter-of-fact tone caused Heather to focus on what she was saying. "You were dreaming." Mrs. Ford touched her shoulder. "You ran off the road in your car. You were attacked and hurt pretty bad."

She looked at her mother in disbelief. "What do you mean? She was right here. I found her and . . ." Heather saw the sadness, worry, and pity etched into her mother's face, and she slowly allowed her reality to sink in.

"For the last week you've been waking up screaming about dogs chasing you." Her mother continued. "Now it's a baby . . ." Mrs. Ford didn't know which was worse: hearing that her only child had been in this horrific accident or sitting for two weeks watching her in and out of consciousness, screaming and fighting images that weren't there. She woke several times but couldn't recognize anyone around her.

"What do you mean? I was robbed?" Heather looked at her hands and the wrap on her leg in disbelief.

"I know you can't remember," her mother touched her hand. "It may be good that you don't. When I got here, you were in ICU because of the seizures. But I prayed to the almighty God because I knew it wasn't your time." Tears fell as she looked at her daughter. "It took some time, but they finally moved you here. The doctor felt it would be better if they kept you asleep because of the seizures."

"Well, good morning, Heather." Heather looked at the short balding man standing on the other side of the bed. "I'm Dr. Bolden." He peered over the top of his glasses and patted her legs reassuringly.

"You gave us quite a scare," he said while inspecting her eyes. "You suffered a major blow to your head, and as a result, your brain suffered damage." Heather could feel the coolness of his hand as he pressed his fingers in the sides of her neck. "The extent of the damage we don't know yet." His voice was low and focused as he continued to check her reflexes. "But you have had several seizures, and we have been working day and night to keep you stable." He touched her hand affectionately. "The baby you've been asking about is a figment of your imagination." He took his glasses off and rubbed his eyes tiredly. "You have been trapped in dreams for the last week, which is a result of the trauma." After a reassuring look at her mother, the doctor smiled. "You are responding very well, but I have added Klonopin to help you get some sleep. How is your head?"

Heather was struggling to take in everything. Her eyes scanned the room. She really was in a hospital, and there was no baby. She looked from her mother, to the nurse, and then at the doctor.

"Heather?" The doctor was calling her name. "Are you hurting? Can you hear me?"

"I hear you, my head is hurting," Heather spoke slow and quietly.

"Okay, we're going to let you get some rest."

Heather felt tears rolling out of the corner of her eyes as she watched the doctor leave. She listened to her mother recount the last two weeks of her life. She couldn't believe how bad she felt. Every part of her body ached, from her head to her legs, even her eyes were throbbing, and the pressure was forcing her to keep them closed.

"You had a lot of visitors." She could hear her mother talking. "Did you see all the balloons and flowers?" Mrs. Ford pointed to all the balloons and cards that took up the corner of the room.

Heather opened her eyes, surprised that she hadn't noticed the color-filled corner. "Janet and Cheri just left about an hour ago. They come by every day. Many of your students, several parents, and a few teachers from your school came by. You'll have to look at the cards because I don't know everyone's name." Mrs. Ford eased down into the chair as if exhausted from telling of the previous day's events. "Two boys from the drama team stopped by."

Heather looked at her mother. "Two?" Her voice was deep and husky.

The boys worked so hard trying to learn their parts, and she let them down. She wished she could talk to them. It hurt her to think they were angry with her. She couldn't help wondering which one hadn't come to visit.

"Oh!" Mrs. Ford jumped up immediately and walked over to a large flower arrangement. "There was this man that came by several times. He was very charming. He brought me lunch every day." Heather opened her eyes immediately. A smile crept in the corner of her mouth. Her head was pounding in her ears as she buzzed for the nurse. She knew that she needed to take something before the pain got too bad.

"Who was he, Mom?" she asked, making sure she kept her voice neutral. It had been two years since she dated anyone seriously. While in graduate school, she had little time to socialize, and after graduating, she dedicated herself to her work at the school.

"I don't know. You got to know him, he's a tall guy, very handsome, he favored Deacon Ellison's son."

Heather rolled her eyes at her mom, wondering why she always made comparisons of people to members of her church, knowing that she never met any of her church members.

"Did he leave a card?" Heather asked tiredly. She watched as her mother walked back over to the flower arrangement. The nurse entered the room with a cup of water and two pills.

Heather took the medicine and quickly laid her head on her pillow.

"He brought these yesterday," Mrs. Ford said, walking over to the flower arrangement sitting on the table. She pulled an envelope from the flowers' grasp and handed it to Heather.

Heather clumsily opened the envelope and pulled out a white card that read, "Praying for you, Ellis Saxton."

"Who is Ellis Saxton?" Heather whispered, handing the paper to her mother as she closed her eyes, trying desperately to will the throbbing pain behind her temple away.

"The detective came by and told me that they had a warrant for the arrest of the guy that attacked you, and to God be the glory, they caught him over the weekend," her mother announced proudly.

Heather could feel the effects of the meds as she drifted off into a dreamless sleep.

Chapter Six

Ellis didn't hide his amusement as Mrs. Ford recounted Heather's reaction to the flowers he had sent up from the gift shop. Since the accident, he struggled to get the image of her out of his mind. Her recovery was slow at first, which allowed him the opportunity to schedule his breaks near the hospital so he could check on her. It was much easier for him when she was taken out of the ICU. He found himself spending most of his breaks in her room, talking with Mrs. Ford.

Standing outside the door, it felt weird to go inside although he had been there countless times before. The realization that Heather has no idea who he is yet he knew everything about her from the meeting with her family, coworkers, and friends was a bit awkward. He smiled to himself and followed Mrs. Ford into the room.

~

Heather was sitting up, eating, when her mother walked in with the man in tow. Her appetite had picked up, and now she was eating anything the nurse put in front of her. She finished eating and began to tune into the conversation her mom was having with the hospital security guard. She actually felt sorry for the guy, knowing he probably had to get back to work, but now he was trapped in a conversation with her mom. Mrs. Ford was talking nonstop about a machine she had purchased online where she could plug in her car to find out if something was wrong with it before she spent money going to a mechanic.

Heather noticed that the man kept looking over at her and felt she had to help him.

"Mom, can you help me move this tray over?" she asked, giving the guy a chance to make his getaway.

Her mother rolled the food tray away from the bed. "Look at how much she ate. I told you her appetite was picking up." Her mom spoke to the man over her shoulder.

Heather watched as the man stepped around her mother and the rolling tray and was purely puzzled when he unzipped his coat and sat down in the chair by the window.

"Oh, Heather." Her mom saw the confused look on her daughter's face. "This is Ellis Saxton. He's the EMT driver that brought you to the hospital."

"Oh!" Heather was completely surprised. "I owe you a debt of gratitude for everything you've done for me," she said, reaching out to shake his hand.

"Yes, you do." Mrs. Ford was eager to validate. "Ellis rode with you to the hospital, and he has stopped by every day." She spoke as if she had known him for years. "He is such a gentleman. He came every day to see if I needed anything."

Heather was amused by her mother's flirting and could see that Ellis was becoming uncomfortable.

"I feel like I already know you," he said shyly as he leaned forward slowly taking her hand. "Your mom has told me so much about you, and she's right. I was pretty worried. I think yours was the worse emergency call I've had. When I came on the scene, and they told me that you had suffered a possible brain injury . . ." He shook his head in disbelief. "I couldn't do anything to help you, so I just rode along and prayed."

Heather watched Ellis as he spoke. She could tell that he was really concerned about her. His dark brown eyes were lit with excitement and fear even as he recounted the story. Her eyes filled with tears as she listened to him. These moments of her life she would never remember. Everything that day seemed to be from a dream; Cheri's party and work that day were a blur, and just thinking that her life could have ended on the side of the road in such a meaningless way was terrifying.

Heather closed her eyes as tears blurred her vision and silence filled the room. Ellis placed a Kleenex in her hand.

"I hope these are tears of joy," he said softly. "You are truly blessed."

His smile was comforting, and she was glad he was there.

~

Heather's recovery was slow. She was plagued with hallucinations that caused troubling dreams, and the doctors told her to expect severe headaches and blurred vision. Dr. Bolden prescribed medication to make life easier for her, but he refused to release her from the hospital until her seizures were under control.

~

After such a lengthy stay in the hospital, Heather was anxious to get her life back. She longed for the normalcy of what her friends called *a boring life*. When the doctor finally released her, she felt the moment was bittersweet. She got her things together as Ellis watched her intently.

"You know I haven't been outside in weeks?" she said, glancing over her shoulder.

She could feel his gaze following her around the room.

"So now the day you've been going on and on about has finally arrived," Ellis said jokingly.

He walked to the window. He realized how convenient her stay had been for him. He stopped by to see her whenever he wanted, many times unannounced. The door was always open. Sometimes he would come early in the morning and bring her mom breakfast; no one thought anything of it. He would sit and talk to her mom just as an excuse to watch her sleep. He didn't have to ask her permission to be a part of her life.

Heather knew Ellis wanted to say something but was hoping he didn't say what she was thinking he was about to say.

"Heather?" Ellis took a deep breath.

Oh no, here it comes, Heather thought to herself.

"You're anxious to leave this place." He motioned around the room. "But I don't want this to be the end." Ellis looked deep into Heather's eyes, hoping she understood what he was saying. The intensity of his gaze forced Heather to look at the floor.

"It's not the end, Ellis." Heather smiled reassuringly. "I am looking forward to getting to know you outside this room," she joked as she indicated the small hospital room, but Ellis knew she was brushing him off.

Heather watched as his expression became veiled and was relieved at her mother's loud laughter as she and the nurse entered the room.

Heather smiled brightly and hugged the nurse as she prepared to walk out.

The nurses were so supportive after watching her slow recovery. Knowing how ready she was to go home, they tried to cheer her up by telling her stories about all the crazy things she said and did. Heather would laugh to tears, but she thought they were mostly exaggerating. She couldn't imagine herself kicking and fighting everyone or doing half of the things they said.

Ellis left the room and returned with a wheelchair.

"What in the world, Ellis! There is no way I'm riding in that thing." Heather was embarrassed by the thought of riding in a wheelchair, knowing she was fully capable of walking.

"I brought you here, and I will take you out!" Ellis said jokingly, but Heather could tell he was a bit reserved.

"Ain't that right, Mama?" He looked at Mrs. Ford as she smiled adoringly at him. He knew he had developed a bond with her that, regardless of how Heather felt, would always be there.

"Heather, sit down," Mrs. Ford insisted. "One day you'll wish you had someone to take the load off your feet." She gently squeezed Ellis's arm as Heather reluctantly sat down in the wheelchair.

"Ellis, I do appreciate everything you've done, especially keeping my mom comfortable." Heather said sincerely. She felt funny as they rolled past a woman walking slow and being assisted by a nurse down the hall. She was relieved when they entered the lobby and she was freed from the wheelchair.

Chapter Seven

In the days following her release, Ellis, true to his words, called every chance he could to check on her. She had to admit she enjoyed his conversation. She hadn't seen him since leaving the hospital, but his calls always seemed to comfort her although he rarely discussed anything other than work.

Heather swallowed the three-pill cocktail that the doctor prescribed as she lay in her bed, looking at the clock with mixed emotions. It was after eleven o'clock and past the time she planned to be asleep to ensure an early start the next morning. She wanted her first day back to go as smoothly as possible, but the excitement and nervousness about seeing everyone and having to answer questions was impeding her ability to rest. Her doctor told her that her new medication would fight off the demons, guaranteeing a restful night, and she was expecting just that. At the hospital, she had the support of the staff, but now that she was home, the thought of having another dreadful dream was scary. She was determined to be consistent with her prescribed regimen.

Heather said a silent prayer as she drifted off to sleep.

~

The first week back flowed seamlessly; the staff stepped in to help Heather catch up with some of the paperwork. After the excitement of her returning diminished and people stopped noticing her each time she entered a room, Heather was able to focus less on her misfortune and more on writing and planning for the drama team.

The aching in her body and stiffening in her legs were her biggest problem physically. Each day, her body, not used to walking and standing, begged her to rest, and by the end of the week, she was walking with a noticeable limp. Heather couldn't wait to get home each day and soak in a hot tub.

Today was no exception as she walked into the house and went straight to the bathroom. Her legs wouldn't carry her much farther. She could tell that her mother had been there as she entered her bedroom and saw that it and the adjoining bathroom had been cleaned. Since being released from the hospital, Mrs. Ford stopped by regularly. Sometimes she left a dinner plate on the stove and washed clothes. A smiled crept onto Heather's tired face as she grabbed a towel from the linen closet; they were folded and stacked neatly by color. She stood a moment in the middle of the bathroom completely exhausted, trying to gather her thoughts.

Heather was glad her mom had left before she arrived. She could imagine the complaining that she would have to endure if her mother saw her barely able to walk after one week of work. She sat on the side of the tub and slowly massaged the throbbing muscles in her legs. She hadn't had any problems with her legs while in the hospital, but now . . .

If it's not one thing, it's another, she thought as she lowered her body into the hot water. Magically the tension started melting away. The heat wrapped around her like a warm blanket, and Heather rested her head against the side of the tub. She fought to keep her eyes open, but soon lost the battle as she drifted off to sleep.

Heather couldn't wait to get back to the house and lie down. Service was over, and she was locking up. Her mind was on the clothes at the house that needed to be washed. She pulled the door open and rushed to the parking lot. In her hurry to get home, one of the doors didn't close all the way. Realizing this, she quickly turned and looked at the door but decided to come back later and lock it.

Two vehicles were left in the parking lot. Neither vehicle belonged to her, but she had the keys to both of them. She felt an overwhelming need to get both vehicles to her house. One of the vehicles was Ellis's. She didn't know how his car had gotten there but was determined to get both cars home.

Her plan was to drive the first car one block, jog back to the church, and get Ellis's car. If she drove his car a block past the first one, she could jog back and get the other car. She planned to do this repeatedly until she got both cars home.

She started driving the other car first. Approaching the first Stop sign, she looked at the road behind her. It didn't seem like she had come far enough to stop to run and get Ellis's car, so she decided to drive another block.

As the car began to pick up speed, she looked at each house as she passed them. Looking to her left, she noticed an alley that she never noticed before. The alley led into a quaint apartment building neatly placed on the lot. A shabby and rotting picket fence surrounded it.

Heather turned her attention back to the road and realized that she had gone through the third Stop sign and Ellis's car was still at the church. She hadn't followed her plan, and now she had arrived at her house.

She entered and immediately went to the washroom to put the load of clothes in the wash, but the basket of clothes was missing.

She walked down a corridor and stopped in front of a closed door. She opened the door and saw the tall basket of white clothes in the middle of the room. As she reached for the basket, she inadvertently knocked it over, and all the clothes spilled over onto the floor.

As she bent to retrieve the clothes, she noticed a red, black, and white stuffed snake underneath. The snake began to move slowly through the clothes. Heather stared at the snake in amazement. She stared at the clothes, trying to figure out how a toy snake was moving by itself. As she moved all the clothes from around it, she discovered a large spider. It was pulling the stuffed snake across the floor with its web.

Heather turned the light on so she could see the spider better. The spider immediately turned into a snake. The real snake grabbed the toy snake and coiled around it. Its fangs were exposed as it stabbed the head of the stuffed snake.

The sound of a crying baby startled Heather. She looked toward the door, wondering where the sound was coming from.

She looked at the floor and saw the snakes had disappeared under the clothes, and the sound of the crying baby was much louder.

It seemed to be coming from the clothes.

Heather reached her hand into the clothes and grabbed the foot of a baby. She pulled the baby from the pile of clothes and saw that it was as naked as a newborn and dripping wet. The water dripped all over the floor. Heather looked at the baby as he was wailing in her arms.

Was this her baby?

The sound of his cry was familiar.

Thinking the baby had been bitten by the snake, Heather took out her cell phone and dialed 911.

She ran from the room and closed the door behind her to keep the snake from getting out.

"What's your emergency?" The operator's voice echoed through the phone.

"I have an emergency, I found a baby in my house, and I think he has been bitten by a snake!" Heather grew frantic. The more she tried to calm the baby, the louder his cries became.

"Is this your baby?" The operator was yelling, trying to be heard over the crying child.

Heather began crying out of frustration and fear. "I don't know." Her voice was muffled as she cried. "I don't know!"

Heather forced her eyes open, immediately realizing her mistake; she had fallen asleep without her medication. She couldn't catch her breath, and the rapid beating of her heart caused her to panic.

Breathe, she silently reminded herself. The thought that stress could trigger a seizure made matters worse.

Breathe! She inhaled and exhaled slowly, leaning over the sink and splashing cold water over her face.

Calm down! she coaxed herself as her body slowly relaxed.

Her heart was still pounding erratically in her chest as she swallowed her meds. She paced the floor in her bedroom, afraid to sit down or lie in her bed for fear of falling asleep before the medicine kicked in. The dreams alone were troubling, but the thought of her accelerated heart rate and heightened anxiety triggering a seizure was more than alarming. For the first time since arriving home, she longed for the safety of the hospital. She could feel the tension rising again in her body.

Without thinking, Heather grabbed the phone and dialed blindly.

After the third ring, Ellis answered.

"Talk to me."

"How did I know you would be up?" she said, hiding the overwhelming relief she felt knowing he was always there when she needed him.

"I'm always up." Ellis turned down the radio and glanced at the clock. "Isn't it past your bedtime?" he asked.

"Yeah, it is past my bedtime, and I am exhausted, but I can't sleep." Heather was breathless but found comfort in Ellis's voice. She lay down on her bed and wrapped her blanket around her.

"Oh yeah? You must be hungry." He laughed, referring to Heather's appetite that Mrs. Ford has started complaining to him about. "Are you okay?"

Heather knew his concern was genuine. "Why are you so sweet, Ellis?"

Ellis laughed out loud. "Sweet! Girl, don't let none of my boys hear you call me sweet," he said jokingly. "I just know when I'm at work, you're asleep, and when I'm asleep, you're pretending to be working."

"Whatever." Heather pretended to be insulted. "I do work."

"Okay, so you probably worked today, but how hard can your job be . . . watching kids run around a stage all day? As a matter of fact, they are the ones working. You just sit there, looking."

"Come on now, my job is much harder than yours because I have to put up with kids and all the extra." Heather defended her job as best she could.

"I guess . . . I'll let you win this argument since you're over there handicapped, hopping around and stuff. Your leg must be giving you problems again?"

"Yeah, a little bit." Heather laughed at his joke, refusing to tell him how sore her legs really were.

"Have the headaches started again?"

"No, not really." Heather knew he would keep fishing until he knew exactly what was bothering her.

"So what's going on?"

"Don't laugh," she said cautiously. "I had a nightmare."

"Why would I laugh?" He sounded insulted. "Heather, you've been through a lot. I'm not sure if you realize it or not, but you had a major head injury, and you're trying to go back to work and get back to a normal routine, but you have to allow yourself time to heal."

Ellis noticed Heather's silence and decided to change his tone. "Okay. Tell me about this horrible dream that chased you into my arms tonight."

Heather gathered her thoughts quickly.

"Your car was parked at this church, and I was trying to drive it and another car to my house." Heather recounted her dream.

"At the same time?" Ellis asked. "How did you pull that off?"

"I didn't. I ended up leaving your car and driving the other one, but when I got home, I saw a toy snake being pulled by this huge spider across the floor, and then the spider turned into a snake and started attacking the toy snake."

"That's a woman," Ellis said quickly.

"How do you know?"

"I heard somewhere that the image of a spider represents a woman's scorn," Ellis said, trying to help in any way he could.

"Okay, what do you think this means?" Heather was eager to hear Ellis's thoughts. "I pull a screaming baby from out of a pile of clothes... It was naked and dripping wet. I think it was covered with urine. I thought the snake had bitten it, but I wasn't sure. I don't know whose baby it was."

Ellis tried to connect the pieces as she recounted the dream.

~

Omar held on to the end table to steady himself. He looked at his reflection in the mirror and laughed. "Who said I couldn't make it?" Everyone thought he would get his third DUI tonight, but they were wrong. He walked into the small bathroom and turned on the shower. He placed his pants clumsily on the cleaner rack and checked his gators for scratches. As he emptied his loose change in the jar on his dresser, he noticed a piece of paper with the name *Heather* scribbled on it. He quickly tossed the paper along with the other trash from his pockets into the trash and jumped in the shower.

Omar could feel his high diminishing as the cold water hit his face. Stepping from the shower, he grabbed a towel and went to the kitchen to get a drink. His mind wandered as he took a long swig of beer.

"Heather?" he thought out loud.

He walked back into the bedroom, and after fumbling around the trash to retrieve the number, he grabbed the phone and dialed quickly.

~

Ellis relaxed in the driver seat, listening as Heather described her dream. The pure emotion that she expressed as she relived the dream made it easy to forget that her experience wasn't real.

He watched the monitor on the dash. A couple of hours had passed since his last call.

"Heather, listen, you need to stop doing this to yourself. There is nothing to figure out. You are having bad dreams because you had a serious head trauma."

"You don't understand." Heather felt exhausted. "It was so real."

"You know how many people have weird dreams after they get hit upside the head!" he said, not realizing he was raising his voice, and the friendly conversation had turned to an argument.

"You're not listening, Ellis," Heather said, losing patience. "A baby is dying. I see it every night, repeatedly I have to know what it means."

Heather heard a beep in her ear. "Is that your dispatch calling?" she said before realizing it was her call waiting indicator. "What time is it?"

"After one," Ellis responded blindly.

Heather wondered who would be calling her at this late hour and decided not to answer, but wonder soon turned to worry.

"Hold on a second," she said before clicking over.

~

"Hello?" Heather answered the phone cautiously. The strange dreams were causing her to expect the worse.

"Hello!" she repeated after hearing silence.

"Hi," Omar said quietly.

"Hello?" Not recognizing the voice, she breathed a sigh of relief; it was obviously a wrong number.

"Yes, is this Heather?" Omar's voice was barely a whisper.

Heather sat up, surprised to hear her name called. "No. May I ask who's calling?"

"Yes, can you tell her that a very close friend would like to speak with her?" Omar replied coyly.

Heather was dumbfounded. "Hold on a second." She had no idea who this person was.

Puzzled, she clicked the line back over to Ellis.

"Hey, Ellis?" she said, not sure if he was still on the line.

"I'm here. Is everything okay?" Ellis replied drily to mask his curiosity about her late-night call.

"Yeah, everything's fine, but I'm going to go." Heather was surprised how the hours had slipped away. She had mistakenly attributed her grogginess to the medication and not the late hour.

"I reckon you're not getting paid to sit on the phone all night," she said jokingly.

"I reckon so," Ellis responded on cue but couldn't believe she was brushing him off again. "I know you got to get your beauty rest."

Heather could hear distance in his voice. "I'll talk to you later, okay."

~

Heather clicked over reluctantly.

"Heather?" Omar was seconds from hanging up.

"Yes, may I ask who's calling?"

"This is a close friend of yours," Omar spoke as seductively as possible.

"Okay, I don't know who this is, but this is not the time for guessing games," Heather said tiredly.

Omar laughed. She still had the same feistiness he remembered from their dance months ago. "Okay. Calm down, you're right. This is Maury, I met you a couple of months ago, and I wanted to hear the voice of a beautiful lady, so I called you."

"Excuse me?" Heather couldn't believe that she thought this was a legitimate call. "Ugh! Mar-ee, or whatever your name is, do you know what time it is? I am so sorry, but you chose the wrong voice to hear tonight." Heather did not hide her annoyance as she hung up the phone.

Chapter Eight

Heather was thankful for her small office as she sat at her desk, sipping her coffee, trying to replenish the energy that had left immediately after her first class. *Thank God for Fridays*, she thought to herself.

"Ms. Ford." Sister Nena's matter-of-fact greeting preceded her as she stepped through the door without knocking.

"Sister Nena? What can I do for you?" A bit startled, Heather forced a smile as she sat her coffee on her desk.

"I came to remind you to submit your surveys before you leave today." Sister Nena looked at the pile of papers on Heather's desk. "I am sure you are aware that they were due some weeks ago, and that being a private institution, we rely heavily on private funding, and our funders rely heavily on those surveys." She gazed unwaveringly at Heather.

"Yes, Sister." Heather felt her hands starting to sweat. "I am aware that the surveys are past due, but I've been trying to catch up on so much since I came back that I seem to have overlooked the surveys."

Sister Nena's gaze was unsympathetic, and her tone was harsh. "I do understand, Ms. Ford, but I placed the reminder in your mailbox on two occasions in the last week. Did you receive the reminders?"

Heather looked at Sister Nena tiredly, trying to think of the best answer to satisfy her. "Well, yes, I did but—"

Sister Nena dismissed Heather quickly by waving her hand in the air. "Ms. Ford, I am very concerned about your commitment to our program. It seems to me that even before your accident you were not giving us 100 percent."

Startled by the sister's bluntness, Heather stood and looked at her watch. "Sister Nena, as you know, I work my tail off with these girls. I even made last-minute adjustments to our schedule to fit in boys from the community. We have an excellent drama program as a result of my contributions, and from what I hear from the community, no one is complaining. The boys were familiar enough with the stage and knew their lines, they pulled it off." Heather walked toward her door, hoping the sister would follow her.

"Forgive me if I don't sound as enthused by your *work*, but it is my opinion that the performance at that ceremony seemed to be the same performance from the summer festival. I was not impressed. Had it not been for the boys, I don't think it would have made the front page." Not only did she not move, she made no effort to leave Heather's office.

Heather didn't have the energy to argue. "You're right," she said quietly. "I wish we had more time to make changes to the program, but we were swamped with the new schedule, and I wanted to give the boys an opportunity to show their talents to their families and to the mayor . . . they worked so hard . . . and the girls . . . I wanted them to do well."

Sister Nena ignored Heather's response. "I am aware that you have had a difficult year, Ms. Ford." Heather nodded a response and listened intently for what seemed to be nonexistent sincerity. "But you have to show me that you want this job. Were you on time today?"

"No, ma'am. I had a long . . ." Heather struggled to get the words out, being completely caught off guard by the question.

"I don't want any more excuses." Sister Nena clapped her hands together loudly. "I want 100 percent, Ms. Ford, and I want those surveys on my desk before you leave today."

Heather picked up her bag to leave but opened the door politely for Sister Nena to pass through.

"Where are you going?" Sister Nena's voice echoed loudly down the empty hall.

"Sister Nena," said Heather, who couldn't hide her frustration any longer, "I have a class that I am trying to get to. Now if you would excuse me . . ." Heather left the sister standing in the doorway and walked toward the auditorium. As she walked down the hall, she could feel the sister's hot gaze on her back.

~

When she entered the auditorium, she saw several students on the stage already working on their impromptu speeches, while others were sitting and talking. She tossed her bag on the chair and called everyone to the front of the stage, but before she could get started, there was another interruption.

"Ms. Ford?" the secretary's voice echoed loudly through the auditorium's intercom.

"Yes?" Heather hushed the students while raising her voice to be heard.

"You are needed in the office," the secretary stated dryly.

"I have a class right now. Can it wait until after class?" Heather looked at the students still getting in place on the stage.

"Send your students to the computer lab and report to the office." The secretary's matter-of-fact voice irritated Heather further.

The students mumbled as they gathered their items together.

Heather grabbed her purse, completely dumbfounded by the direction the day had taken.

Before going to the office, she stopped by the lounge to check her hair in the mirror. She wanted to look presentable for the parent that was probably waiting. Sister Nena never kept parents waiting or any visitor for that matter. She didn't mind pulling teachers from class to show parents and visitors that they are the most important factor.

Heather stopped in the mail room to check her box, not surprised to see that it was overflowing with memos and notices.

"Where's the fire?" she asked Sister Shell, the school's secretary.

"There's no fire, Ms. Ford." Sister Shell handed her a thick yellow envelope. "Sister Nena wants you to go ahead and work on these surveys."

Heather could feel the heat moving slowly up the back of her neck. "I just talked to her, why would she pull me from class for this? I thought she needed them by the end of the day."

She looked at the thickness of the envelope, which was twice the size of the surveys she had waiting on her desk. "What is this?" she said, throwing the envelope on the counter, ripping it open.

Sister Shell came around her desk and leaned across the counter. "She canceled all your classes until you get this done," she whispered as she handed Heather a "while you were out" notice. "She's not happy. Just get it done."

Heather looked at the concerned look in the nun's eyes, and her anger dissipated. *I have to do better*, she thought to herself as she looked at the small paper in her hand.

"You had three phone calls." The sister was speaking quietly so no one could overhear her. "I was going to come get you after the third call, but the caller said it was not an emergency." She paused, looking intently at Heather. "You are aware that you are not allowed personal calls in the office?"

Heather grabbed the yellow envelope and turned to leave the office.

"Yes, Sister Shell, I am aware of that, but thank you."

As soon as she closed her office door, she pulled out her cell phone. She dialed the number from the paper, and while waiting for someone to pick up, she pulled the surveys from the envelope.

"Hello, Omar Eden speaking."

"Yes, Mr. Eden, this is Heather Ford returning your call."

"Oh . . . Ms. Ford," Omar replied after a brief pause. "I work with UIA Investment and Insurance Company. I ran into your friend Cheri, and she gave me your contact information. I was told that you are looking for information about investing in an IRA."

"I am." Heather was looking at all the paperwork in front of her. "Mr. Eden, I would like to talk with you, but I am at work, and this is not the best time."

"I understand. When would be a better time for you?" Omar smiled while maintaining his professionalism.

"Today is just not a good day," Heather responded while organizing the surveys.

"Okay, what about Saturday around noon?" He spoke quickly to let her know that he was not trying to take too much of her time.

"Okay, that sounds great," Heather said, writing the appointment on a yellow Post-it. "Would you like to meet somewhere?"

"Sure, that will be great." Omar could hardly contain himself.

He ran into Cheri when he stopped at Danvers on his way to work. He gave her his card as a potential client, not really wanting to bring up Heather since he had pissed her off the night before. Cheri asked him if he had spoken with Heather since she worked at a privately funded school that didn't have a 401K. He didn't think it would be this easy to convince her to meet him for lunch.

"Are you familiar with the Internet café in the town square?" Heather knew they had meeting rooms that usually were available on Saturdays.

"Yeah, sure, that sounds good, noon Saturday," Omar repeated.

"See you then," Heather said curtly before hanging up the phone.

Heather looked at the clock and saw that it was almost nine thirty. Judging by the number of surveys that were in front of her, Heather knew she would be there until the end of the day.

~

"I see you made it!" her mom yelled from the kitchen as she walked into the house.

"Hi, Ma," Heather replied, throwing herself onto the couch while massaging her temples, trying to find the right spot to numb the pain for the throbbing headache. She could hear her mother's shoes sliding across the floor as she rushed into the living room where she was sprawled across couch.

"What's wrong? Are you hurting?"

Before Heather could reply, Mrs. Ford was running to get a blanket from the closet.

"I told you it was too early for you to go back to work, you should have been out at least a couple months to allow yourself to recover." Mrs. Ford was pushing the blanket into the crease of the couch pillows. "The doctor said ninety days, but you just won't listen."

"Mom, you're hurting me!" Heather complained as her mother pushed a pillow behind her head. "It's not the accident that's giving me problems, it's this job. I can't seem to catch up, and Sis Nena is riding my back every day." Heather felt the weight of the day wrap her body tighter than the blanket that was now impeding her movement.

"You wouldn't believe my day. If I could just work with the kids and forget all the 'extra,' I would be okay." Heather kicked the blanket off her legs and walked into the washroom.

"This woman took me out of my class for the whole day so that I could fill out about a hundred surveys!" Heather yelled. "Oh, but check this out, she burst in my office, talking bout I ain't giving them 100 percent, and my attendance is poor." She looked at her tearstained face in the mirror, thinking, *This is my reality, and there isn't a thing I can do about it, so why complain.*

She emerged from the bathroom after her nightly regimen and made a beeline to her bedroom.

"You have to eat, Heather," her mother said, following her with a dinner plate.

She watched as Heather sat on the side of the bed tiredly before handing her the plate.

"Heather, are you taking care of yourself?" she asked hesitantly.

"I'm okay, Mom, I just need to find some kind of balance." Heather smiled, reassuring her mother as she ate the food before her.

"You should think about coming to church with me. You need to be around people who can pray with you and help you get through all this."

Heather listened as her mother gave her what now was becoming a routine speech ever since she stopped attending church regularly.

"I have so much going on right now, Mama." She looked up and saw the sad, almost pleading expression on her mother's face and stopped talking.

"I'll try to come Sunday."

Chapter Nine

Omar parked and walked through the town center. The sun was out and so were the people. He admired the quaint café tucked away in the cove. The fact that it wasn't in a high traffic area worked to his advantage because he never brought a potential client to a crowded environment.

He found a table in the corner large enough to hold a comfortable meeting. He took out his laptop and began setting the table with pamphlets and visuals that he felt would impress Heather. UIA (United Investment Associations) was one of the top performing investment companies in the United States and was recently featured in *Forbes Magazine*. Omar was hoping that this and the fact that he was the top broker in the state would impress Heather.

"So you're with UIA?"

Omar turned to greet a young woman standing behind him.

"That is correct," he replied, handing the woman a business card. He noticed her freshly manicured hands. "Are you familiar with UIA?"

She smiled and moved a loose hair from her face. "I can be."

Omar looked at the young woman, not surprised by her forwardness. Another day and time he would have played the game with her, but he was here on business. "Okay, take my card. I'm always looking for serious investors." Omar turned away from the woman, hoping she would take the hint.

~

Heather finished her shopping at the shoe store that was only a couple of doors down from the café. She looked at her watch as she walked quickly up the sidewalk, hoping Mr. Eden hadn't been waiting long.

"Ms. Ford?" The now familiar voice called her name when she stepped through the door.

Omar walked toward Heather, knowing the strange woman was still standing at his table, waiting on him. He braced himself for Heather's reaction when she saw his face and realized who he was. *She is definitely going to think I'm a creep after that early morning call*, he thought. He decided that sticking to the business model was the best way to go. His anticipation left as he focused on Heather "the client" and not as the beautiful woman that he wanted to get acquainted with.

Heather looked at Omar as he approached her and smiled. "Omar Eden?" she asked politely, shaking his hand as he walked her toward the table.

Omar was surprised by her reaction. He expected a catfight in the café, but she acted as if she really didn't recognize him.

"I'll pick up a few of these," the woman said to save face as he approached the table with Heather in tow.

"Okay, just give me a call and let me know what you think." He maintained his professionalism by politely flashing a smile as the lady walked away.

"You must be really busy." Heather said, referring to his apparent clientele. The young lady was flawless. Heather noticed that she sported this season's Michael Kors handbag and matching boots.

Heather turned her attention to Omar Eden. She felt she had met him somewhere before, but she wasn't sure where. He was distinguished and sexy. She looked at his polished shoes and custom suit and concluded that he held his own financially. She glanced at his hand. No ring. He's either available, in a relationship, or gay. *Which one it is?* she thought.

She noticed Omar looking at her.

"Is something wrong?" he asked.

"No. Nothing's wrong. Have we met before?"

Omar decided to change the subject. "We all have a twin somewhere." He laughed.

"Let's look at some numbers." He immediately turned to the presentation board that he had provided for her. "Are you familiar with our company?" He changed the subject smoothly, relieved and somewhat disappointed that she had no clue who he was.

"I am." Heather smiled as she took out her notepad and pen.

Omar began his presentation with a slide show that told her about the company and the founders. He gave her a brief list of the major investors. He noticed that Heather was listening intently to every word while taking notes. Every now and then, she would ask a question that showed him she had done her research, and she wasn't wasting his time. He gave her several brochures that explained in detail each type of account and the average return for the last fifteen years.

"So how do you manage your time?" Heather asked innocently.

"I stay pretty busy." Omar paused momentarily. "I have several agents that work the field, but if our numbers start dropping, then I come out of the office and . . ." He smiled. "Here I am."

Omar went ahead and concluded his presentation. He proudly announced that he was the top broker in the state and that his clients were satisfied with the return they were receiving on their investments.

"Do you have any questions, Ms. Ford?" he said as he closed the laptop.

"I'm impressed," Heather replied honestly. She hadn't expected to be presented with such a thorough presentation by such a handsome man. "This is a lot of information, and I need to take some time to look over the numbers, but I will definitely get back with you."

Omar knew the meeting was a success when he wrote Heather's name on his callback calendar. When Heather started gathering her things, he decided to try to detain her.

"This seems to be a nice place, do you come here often?" he asked.

Heather smiled inwardly. *Small talk, really?* she thought, easing her purse back onto the table.

"I do. They have very good food. Have you eaten?" she smiled innocently, knowing if he accepted the invitation to eat, he was all hers.

"No, I actually could use a bite. Do you mind?" he spoke while loosening his tie so she could see that he planned to relax. "So how do you manage *your* time?"

The minutes quickly turned to hours. Lunch was cleared, and the wine arrived. Heather was intrigued as Omar told her of his travels and laughed as he did impressions of many of the people he met along the way. He listened to her laughter and watched her expression change time and time again. He told many stories from his past, some true and some he made up as he went along, but it didn't matter as long as he made her smile. He listened as she talked about her job that she apparently hated and her mom, whom she adored. Then suddenly, she became quiet.

"Is something wrong?" he asked, not sure why her mood suddenly changed.

"No. Well, yes . . ." She watched him intently. "I just realized something." Heather cleared her throat. She didn't realize how much the accident had taken out of her. She couldn't remember the last time she came out and actually enjoyed herself. She wanted to say that she was having the time of her life, but she smiled and decided against it.

"I had the worst night of my life right before Thanksgiving last year," Heather said uncomfortably, but since she had no recollection of those three weeks, she decided to recount her statement. "Let me change that, I was *told* that it was the worst night of my life."

"What do you mean?" Omar asked, not sure where Heather was going with the conversation.

Heather realized that this was her first time telling someone about the accident who wasn't already familiar with it. "I was in a really bad car accident," she said.

Omar looked at Heather in total confusion. She didn't look like she had been hurt in an accident.

"What happened?" he asked.

"Coming home from a party last November, I had a blowout, which caused me to wreck."

Omar stared at Heather in total shock. "This happened before Thanksgiving?"

His mind went back to the night he met her. He vaguely remembered Stephon mentioning something about her tire. "Yeah, it was a couple of weeks before," Heather recounted as Omar shifted uncomfortably in the chair.

He looked at her cautiously. *She couldn't be referring to that night, could she?*

"You had a flat on the way home from the party?"

"Not just a flat . . . I went off the embankment and wrecked my car." Heather smiled at his horrified reaction.

"You wrecked your car?"

"That's not the worse part. I could deal with the flat and the wreck, but sometime afterward, I was apparently attacked and robbed."

"You were robbed?" Omar stared at her in total disbelief. He couldn't believe all this happened that night.

"I was hurt pretty bad and was in the hospital a long time."

Omar quickly put all the pieces together. So that's why she didn't remember him.

"I am so sorry that happened to you," he whispered, taking her hand gently.

Heather was touched by his sincerity. His eyes never left hers, nor did his hand.

"Oh, I'm fine." Heather smiled reassuringly.

"What happened when you went to the hospital? I mean, did they catch whoever did this?"

"Yes, they caught the guy, some poor addict. I was just in the wrong place at the worse time. He got me pretty good with a brick to the head." Heather paused as Omar poured the last of the wine in his glass. She noticed he had emptied the whole bottle.

"It could be worse," she thought out loud.

"And you have no recollection of that day?" he asked, watching her over the top of his glass.

"Nothing," she said matter-of-factly. "I vaguely remember work that day, but it's like images that come and go. I really can't say if they are from that particular day or some other day." She shrugged sadly.

Omar listened to Heather while unconsciously tracing the intricate embroidery of the tablecloth with his finger. "Do the doctors think it's permanent, or will your memory come back?" he asked, never looking up from the cloth, silently relieved that he didn't have to explain the drunken call from the other night.

Heather noticed the change in his posture and his glazed stare and felt that he may have had too much to drink. "I think I can go on for days, Omar, but I think it's time for both of us to get home." She smiled as she beckoned for the waiter.

"No, stay just a bit longer, please?" He smiled charmingly, knowing that most women couldn't resist his smile.

Heather was taken aback by his childlike demeanor, thinking how much different he was from the man that she met two and a half hours ago. "I have to go." She smiled graciously and picked up her purse. "We have to do this again."

"Okay, Ms. Ford," Omar said, pronouncing her name completely and sarcastically. He smiled inwardly, remembering the expression on her face when they met that night in the parking and he said her name.

"Where did you park?" he asked as they left the restaurant.

Heather smiled politely. "You don't have to walk me, I'm fine." She hesitated before turning to leave. "Will you be okay driving?" She didn't hide her concern.

"No, I'm fine, Heather." He grinned at the thought that a bottle of wine would leave him impaired.

"Okay, thank you for the presentation and lunch," Heather said, shaking his hand firmly.

"I'll give you a call next week," he said as Heather turned and walked across the parking lot.

~

As soon as Heather got in her car, she hit the call button on her steering wheel.

"Who would you like to call?" the male voice rang from the dashboard.

"Call Cheri." Heather loved her new car. She traded in her Camry, which was a constant reminder of the accident, for her Altima before going back to work.

"Calling Cheri..."

Cheri's phone rang loudly through the car.

"And where are you going?" Cheri answered, recognizing Heather's mobile number on her caller ID.

"What do you mean?" Heather laughed. She hadn't heard her good friend's voice in weeks. "Why do I have to be going somewhere?" she said mysteriously.

"Okay then, where are you coming from?"

Cheri was canvassing the neighborhood of the property that she was planning to list for her new client when Heather called.

"I met with Mr. Eden this morning for that presentation." Heather reached into her bag and pulled out one of the pamphlets. "He was quite impressive."

"Okay, tell me about Mr. Eden." Cheri parked the car in front of a house with a For Sale sign in the yard. She was glad to hear the excitement in Heather's voice. She was starting to worry about her. After the accident, she hadn't come to any of the outing with the girls.

Heather smiled. "The presentation was quite convincing, but you could have warned me about him."

Cheri got out of the car and walked to the sign in front of the house to get the printout of the home's description from the drop box. "Warned you about who?" she asked, not sure what Heather was talking about.

"About your friend . . . Omar!" Heather said, reaching in her purse for the business card she took off the table. Heather paused, realizing she hadn't asked Cheri if she was available to talk. "You must be busy?"

"No, I can talk. I'm not doing any showings today, it's just that I'm confused because you never mentioned an Omar Eden before." Cheri looked at the paperwork as she drove away from the house.

"You know, the guy that works for UIA, the investment company, very tall sexy, pretty smile, clean-cut?" Heather described Omar as best she could.

"Nope, don't know him," Cheri said quietly as she updated her logbook. "You must really like him?"

"What do you mean? You referred him to me, to help diversify my portfolio, remember?" Heather was impatiently pleading with Cheri to try and remember.

Cheri thought for a second. "Oh, I know who you're talking about, your friend from the club."

"My friend?" Heather was sure Cheri was mistaken. Omar looked familiar to her, but she would have known if he was someone she knew. "How is he my friend?"

"Yeah, that was the guy you danced with at my birthday party the night of the accident. He was a real charmer." Cheri remembered how much fun she had that night and the horror that took place early the next morning when she got the call that Heather had been in the accident.

"I knew he looked familiar, but I don't remember anything from that night." Heather was stunned. "Are you sure? Because he didn't mention anything about that."

"Well, I saw him in McDonald's the other day and recognized him from the party. He spoke and handed me his business card. When I saw that it was dealing with financial planning, I asked him if he had spoken to you about it. I mentioned that you worked at a private school that didn't offer many options," Cheri explained. "I thought you were friends, that's why I gave him your information."

"No, he called me at work and told me that he was a friend of yours and that you had referred me. I simply scheduled the appointment to meet him this morning. When I saw him, I thought he looked familiar. I'm not sure if he remembered me either because he didn't act like he knew me."

"Maybe he didn't remember you, and when I said that my friend Heather was interested, he just called you, not knowing who you were either," Cheri said thoughtfully. "It's amazing how you guys met for the first time twice. This may be a good sign, girl. Don't lose him again."

Cheri was right; this was a good sign. Heather couldn't understand why Omar hadn't said anything about them meeting before. He seemed to be genuinely upset when she was telling him about that night, or maybe it was the alcohol. It didn't bother her that he had a little too much to drink. She was glad that he was comfortable enough to be himself around her. There was something different about him, but she liked it. His personality intrigued her, and she couldn't wait to find out what was behind his natural smile.

~

Heather pulled up at her mother's house and was surprised to see Ellis out front cutting the grass.

"Hey, stranger!" she yelled over the roar of the mower.

Ellis smiled inwardly when he saw Heather. Each time he stopped by to visit Mrs. Ford, he hoped she would drop by, but she very seldom did. When they talked, it was always on the phone while he was working, and each time he asked her out, she would brush him off as if he was joking.

He cut the mower off and walked over to greet her. Covered in dirt and grass, he smiled sheepishly. "Can I get a hug?"

"You sure can, after you get cleaned up." Heather laughed.

Ellis saw the opportunity and took it. "What about lunch next week?"

Heather pushed Ellis away playfully and walked into the house.

Chapter Ten

Every Saturday night, Omar and his friends got together to play a high stakes game of poker. With thousands of dollars on the table, the tension was high inside, causing Omar and few other guys to take refuge on the front steps. Omar stood, enjoying a smoke in the cool night air when his phone rang and an unknown number appeared.

"Eden," he answered.

"Hello, Mr. Eden, my name is Lana Cunningham. I met you today downtown, I picked up a few of your brochures from a display that you were setting up."

Omar remembered the young woman that approached him when he was setting up for his meeting with Heather. "So now I have a name to put with that beautiful smile."

"Oh, really? You don't sound surprised to hear from me."

"You said you would call, and I like it when a person keeps their word. What can I do for you, Ms. Cunningham, or can I call you Lana?"

"Lana is fine."

"Well, Lana, you have my attention." Omar retrieved his appointment calendar on his phone.

"Mr. Eden, you seem like an approachable guy, and I like that."

"Thank you, Lana, it's not often that I hear that." Omar laughed. "When is a good time for you?

"How about now?" Lana said bluntly. "I would like to meet with you so we can talk . . . off the clock?"

Omar knew where the conversation was headed. He looked through the window at the guys sitting around the table. He really didn't want to step out in the middle of a card game.

"Yes, I am most definitely off the clock, what is it you need to talk about?" Omar knocked on the window and beckoned for Stephon to come out. When the door opened, the music flooded onto the breezeway. Omar grabbed Stephon and pulled him out of the door, silencing the loud noise.

"Get my keys off my nightstand," Omar whispered.

"I'm not sure." Lana paused, contemplating how to start the conversation. She could hear a lot going on in the background. "Did I catch you at a bad time? Because you can call me back."

"You know what? Let me take care of something, and I'm going to call you right back," Omar said reluctantly.

~

Omar ran in his room to find Stephon rummaging through his drawer. "I said on the nightstand, dude." He pushed Stephon aside and reached in the drawer of the nightstand and retrieved his keys.

"Well, that sure as hell ain't *on* the nightstand. That looks like *in* the nightstand to me." Stephon pushed Omar, causing him to fall over the side of the lounge chair behind him. Omar fell to the floor and jumped up quickly, grabbing Stephon in a choke hold.

"Say *Big Papa*, and I'll let go," Omar said as he tightened his grip around Stephon's neck.

He was well aware that he could overpower Stephon.

Stephon mumbled through clenched teeth until he felt his breath shortening and the room beginning to spin. "Okay. *Okay! Big Papa,*" he said quickly, tapping Omar's upper arm and falling to the floor.

"That's what I'm talking about, Playa." Omar flexed his muscles as he walked into the bathroom.

Looking in the mirror, he couldn't help but smile at the day's turn of events. He wasn't surprised that Lana wanted to have a "conversation" off the clock. He had that effect on women. If he could get them to give him five minutes, they come back begging for a whole day, and some like Lana come looking for a late dinner and a long night.

He stepped out of the bathroom and noticed Stephon still sitting on the floor where he left him.

"I need you to do me a favor." Omar took his casual blazer from his closet. "I need you to lock up for me when everyone leaves. I'm stepping out for a minute."

He walked over and helped his friend up from the floor.

"You all right?" he said, noticing Stephon was swaying slightly. "You drunk already?"

He looked at Stephon, hoping he wouldn't pass out before he locked the house up.

"Don't worry about me, I'm good." Stephon laughed while visibly straightening his posture.

"Ease up on the liquor tonight, I need you to watch the house for me." Omar couldn't hide his concern. Stephon assured him as he pushed him out the front door.

"I got this," he said as he watched his friend leave.

~

Mrs. Ford convinced Ellis to stay and eat before he left. They sat around the table, laughing and talking until the sun went down, and Ellis left in a hurry when he looked at the time and realized he hadn't checked in at work.

"You need to stop playing hard, Heather, and let him take you out. He talks about you all the time," her mother was saying as they finished cleaning the kitchen and sat down to watch Steve Harvey on *Family Feud*.

Heather sighed tiredly. "I should," she agreed with her mother. "I'm just not attracted to him in that way. Plus . . ." Heather laid her head back, pretending to fall asleep. "I met someone."

Heather smiled. Even with her eyes closed, she could feel her mother's piercing glare on her face.

"Who?" Mrs. Ford said sharply.

"His name is Omar, and I think you're going to like him," Heather spoke with closed eyes.

"I don't remember you mentioning him before. How do you know him?"

Heather sat up, thrilled to finally be able to tell someone about Omar.

"That's the thing, Mama, I met him the night of the accident, and again the other day."

Mrs. Ford responded cautiously, "The night of the accident? In a club?"

Heather could see the dismay in her mother's expression and decided her mother wasn't the best person to talk to about Omar. She laid her head back again and pretended to be falling back asleep.

Mrs. Ford watched as Heather pretended to sleep—an avoidance tactic that she was fully aware of. It had been two years since her husband passed away, and he too would pretend to be asleep when he didn't want to talk to her. She decided not to push the issue and instead reached over and touched her daughter's knee gently.

"Heather, please be careful. There are men out there that will take advantage of you."

She wanted to share her excitement, but she couldn't understand why, with a good man like Ellis around, Heather would fall for a man she met in a club. It wasn't until she heard snoring that she realized that Heather really was sleeping.

Heather watched the road intently as a car passed her on the highway.

Janet looked out the window and screeched loudly, "Heather, did you see that?"

"See what?" Heather asked, trying to look over her shoulder.

"There was a church on fire. Wait till we go up the bridge, you should be able to see it then."

Heather began driving over the bridge that looped around the city. As they went higher on the bridge, she scanned the skyline for signs of smoke as Janet had suggested, but she didn't see anything. As she came off the bridge, she saw what appeared to be a brick building that was not a church, but the bushes in front were burning.

Janet stared in confusion because she was sure the fire was much larger and that it was a big church. She turned and looked out the back window to see if she saw the church somewhere else.

As Heather took the exit ramp and prepared to stop at a light, she noticed a patch of grass burning on the corner. When she turned, she saw several small fires along the sidewalk in front of businesses and homes.

"Do you know what's going on?" Heather turned to Janet. "I think this is a brush fire like the ones they have out west. We need to get to the house and get our things before it gets worse."

Heather turned onto a treelined street that appeared to be a historical district with large brick homes. There were no signs of the fire as they pulled in front of the house. They both jumped from the car and ran up on the porch, calling out to anyone listening. As they ran through the house, Heather noticed there were a lot of kids there. She told them to grab what they could and soon began pushing them out the front door. On the porch, she could see that the first three houses on the street were engulfed in flames, and the bushes in front of the house next door were burning.

"Everyone out!" she yelled "The fire is here!"

There were so many children. They ran past Heather with their arms full of personal items.

"Go to the street!" Heather yelled as she ran back into the house to make sure everyone was out.

She ran from one room to the other until she came to her mother's room. There, her fifty-nine-year-old mother sat in a rocking chair with a small infant in her arms. A pink-and-white cloth was placed over the head of the infant, and she appeared to be breast-feeding.

Heather stood, wondering how her mother was able to provide milk for the baby that was not her baby and at her apparent age. At that moment, Janet entered the room and asked the question that Heather was thinking.

Mrs. Ford looked at them calmly. "He has been in my presence long enough for my body to respond to his needs by making the milk necessary for him to survive. Be patient," she spoke quietly. "If he doesn't receive nourishment, he won't make it."

Heather wasn't sure how long she had been asleep, but she sat for a moment, thinking. Why was everything burning? Just like every dream since the accident, a baby was on the brink of death, but this time, the baby wasn't alone when she found it. Heather thought about what her mother's reaction would be when she'd tell her that she was breastfeeding a baby in her dream.

After being haunted night after night for three months by a dying baby, Heather felt like a load had been lifted. The baby wasn't dying this time. It looked healthy and was getting what it needed to survive. Heather wondered what it meant. Was it over? The feeling of relief was overwhelming.

~

Omar navigated his way around the cars that were parked precariously in the driveway. As soon as he pulled onto the street, he dialed Lana's number.

"I thought you had forgotten about me," Lana said.

Omar laughed. "Oh, am I *not* moving fast enough for you? What's on your mind?" Omar knew she was the type that only operated in the fast lane.

"I don't know . . . I just wanted to chill, you know."

Omar knew exactly what she wanted. He decided to meet her at a private spot he and his friends frequented with private dining and bar. She was waiting in the parking lot when he arrived. Her car of choice was an Audi Coupe, and she waited patiently for him to open the door for her. When she stepped from the car, Omar couldn't believe he hadn't noticed how sexy she was in their first meeting.

As expected, she took control of the evening, ordering her drink and his. She started the conversation, but didn't really participate in it. Omar found himself talking more than usual while she drank, not really listening. "Do you like working in finance?" she asked as the waiter filled her glass. "It seems like it can be a bit taxing."

"By taxing, do you mean boring?" Omar smiled at her lack of interest.

"It can be 'boring' at times until you meet that one person." He sipped his wine and decided to make the conversation more to her liking. "It's the challenge. I find out what my clients want, and I make sure they get it."

"Really? What happens when you can't deliver?"

"I always deliver."

"What if the client is not interested?"

"If I want them bad enough, I go after them." He looked at her intently. "It's the thrill of the chase, Ms. Cunningham."

"Who's chasing who, Mr. Eden?" Lana's gaze never wavered.

Omar was impressed by her tenacity but felt it was time to let her know who she was dealing with. "I'm scheduled to meet with the CEO of Dukes & Duchess next week," he stated offhandedly. D&D was a new multimillion-dollar design and distribution company that had every marketing and investment firm fighting to secure a contract. To have an appointment with the CEO was a major accomplishment, and Omar new it.

"That's is quite impressive," Lana said dismissively, grabbing her purse. "I'm going to head to the powder room."

Irritated by her rudeness, Omar watched as Lana made her way through the crowd. He didn't have the energy to entertain and had no qualms about changing his mind about the evening. Omar decided he was ready to head home as he picked up the tab and waited for her to reappear.

Omar had little to say as they walked toward the parking lot.

Lana watched Omar's forlorn expression. Thinking about how easily he dismissed her when she met him in the café earlier when she was showing him interest, and now he was ready to dismiss her again because she wasn't showing enough interest.

"I know Dave very well, I'll put in a good word for you," she said, starting the engine, and cutting his good-night speech short.

"Who is Dave?" Omar asked confused.

"You said you had a meeting with the CEO of Dukes & Duchess." She was amused by his surprised expression. "His name is David Baine, and I'll put in a good word for you." She handed him her GPS. "Put in your address. I can use that nightcap."

Omar stared at her in disbelief. *What did she mean when she said that she knew him very well?* He keyed in his address.

Lana looked at the distance to his house with obvious dismay. "You live twenty minutes away, but I live right around the corner."

Omar was speechless as a slow smile crept across his face. He wasn't sure if she was playing games with him or not, but there was only one way to find out.

"Your place it is," he said, flashing his million-dollar smile.

Chapter Eleven

Heather awoke early to the sound of birds as the sun peeked through the window. She felt an overwhelming sense of contentment as she sat on the side of the bed, thinking about the day ahead. She had promised her mother that she would pick her up for worship service this morning, and she knew she couldn't be late.

While in the shower, she began to reflect on her luncheon the previous day. She felt relaxed with Omar, and he seemed really relaxed with her. She wanted to see him again. He seemed approachable. What would he say if she asked him out?

Heather dressed quickly and rushed over to pick up her mother.

~

Her thoughts were miles away as she entered the church, but she quickly became engulfed in well wishes and hugs, which forced her to focus on the people gathering around her. Feeling a bit awkward, Heather escaped to the sanctuary, hoping that she wouldn't have to stand and introduce herself, which seemed to be a practice at every church she visited.

A girl in her early teens walked to the front of the church and, without hesitation, started to sing. Heather was taken off guard by the strength in the young girl's voice. The words from the song spilled from her lips and flowed effortlessly through the air. One song after another, Heather listened as the young voice joined with the choir, providing beautiful songs with melodies that soothed her. She found herself relaxing. The selections from the choir were also mesmerizing, and without much thought, she was clapping her hands with everyone around her.

When the pastor was introduced, the ushers took their seats, and a pregnant silence replaced the musical instruments. Heather watched as he approached the podium with the assistance of the other men in the pulpit. He didn't appear to be in much of a hurry as he moved seemingly in slow motion. Heather sighed deeply while searching her purse for something to write on and mentally prepared herself for a long sermon as the elder placed his Bible and notes down gingerly on the podium.

"Mother Ford?" His baritone voice broke the silence. "A battle is raging."

"Amen, Pastor," Mrs. Ford, who was sitting on a corner pew with the other church mothers, chimed in with those of the congregation.

"John 10:10 says that the thief comes to steal and to kill and to destroy, but I come that they might have life and have it more abundantly." He organized the notes in front of him and deliberately placed his glasses on his face.

"Sister Heather, it's a blessing to see you, daughter."

Heather was not surprised when she heard her name and felt comforted by his words.

"When you were in the hospital, fighting for your life, the devil thought he had you, but God blocked him."

"Amen, Pastor," Heather said in agreement.

~

The ride home was filled with Mrs. Ford recounting every part of the service, from the opening announcements to the benediction and closing prayer. Heather realized that the church was becoming her mother's life. She recalled how worried she was when her father passed away, not sure how her mother would manage in the house alone when everyone left and the phones stopped ringing. In the beginning, it was hard, but as the months passed, Heather watched as her mother submerged herself in missionary work and found healing for herself while serving others. She lost herself in making sure the needs of the pastor were met and all auxiliaries were up to par at the church. There was never a dull moment in her life because she spent her morning calling the sick and evenings visiting or meeting with the other mothers. Sometimes they spent the evening washing and ironing choir robes, but for the most part, they just loved to be in each other's company.

Heather looked adoringly at her mother and smiled.

"What's funny?" Mrs. Ford asked, curious about the mysterious grin on her daughter's face.

Heather's grin turned into laughter, causing her mom to laugh as well.

"What?" Mrs. Ford asked, not sure why she was laughing.

"I had another dream last night."

Mrs. Ford watched Heather's expression closely, not sure what to think since Heather's dreams were so disturbing that they avoided talking about them.

"This one was different," Heather said, reading her mother's expression.

"No dying baby?"

"Well, sort of." Heather wasn't sure how to explain it. "There was a baby, but this time when I found it, you were holding it."

Hearing that she was in the dream piqued Mrs. Ford's interest. "I was holding the *dying* baby!"

Heather smiled as she chose her words carefully, making sure she didn't offend her mother. "No, this time the baby wasn't dying. You were holding a fat and healthy baby. Healthy because you were providing it with nutrients through your breast milk."

Her play on words didn't fool her mother. "How was I breast-feeding a baby?" she asked bluntly. "I must've been real young?"

"No, you were the same age you are now." Heather giggled. "You told me that the baby had been around you long enough to trigger hormones in your body, and you were able to make milk to feed it to keep it healthy."

Mrs. Ford was speechless. She considered the mysterious nature of the dream. For a baby to receive nourishment from a woman her age was one thing, but the thought that the baby required food and the fact that her body responded miraculously by making the milk was so profound that she found it troubling. This baby was a survivor, but to what end?

Why was her daughter being drawn into this mystery? An unexplainable sense of dread touched her heart as she looked closely at Heather. Death was near. Her mind went back to the scripture the pastor quoted in today's sermon, John 10:10: the thief comes to steal, kill, and destroy, but the Lord comes that they may have life. She felt an overwhelming need to pray, to bind the devil and whatever he had planned for her daughter. The pastor was right, *a battle was raging.*

~

Heather dialed Omar's number as soon as she dropped her mom off. She couldn't hide her smile when Omar answered the phone.

"Hi, this is Heather Ford. Are you busy?" she asked.

"No, I've been up." Omar sat up and looked at the clock. His eyes were closed, but his mind was working overtime. He made it home at first light and found Stephon drunk on the couch as expected, but the house was intact, and nothing appeared to be broken or missing.

Even after his long night with Lana, the fact that he had made an impression on Heather to the point that she was calling him bright and early on a Sunday was not lost to him.

"Hey, I want to see you," he said without thinking. "Have you eaten? Come over, and I'll cook you brunch."

Heather was relieved that he extended the invitation first because now all she had to do was act surprised and graciously accept. She had already decided that she had been single way too long, and it was time to throw caution to the wind.

"Have my food ready when I get there. Or do you need my assistance?" she said jokingly.

"For sure." Omar was surprised she accepted his invitation. "What, you don't think I can throw down in the kitchen?" Omar pretended to be insulted.

"I hope you can! A single man better know how to cook."

It took a moment before Omar realized that his suggestion wasn't the best idea. He had just made it in after frolicking with Lana all night, Stephon was still passed out on the couch, and the house was in no condition to invite a date too.

"You know what, if I'm going to cook for you, I would rather cook you a nice dinner. Can I give you a rain check and change our lunch date to a dinner date tomorrow evening?"

"Okay, that sounds good, but I will only cash in that rain check for a four-course meal . . . including dessert and white wine . . . *all* prepared by the hands of Chef Omar."

Omar laughed as Heather made her request.

"Six o'clock tomorrow it is."

Chapter Twelve

The blaring sound of the alarm woke Heather early. She bolted from the bed with vigor that she hadn't had all year. She promised herself to be on time, and she planned to stay away from the office as much as possible. Since she completed all the surveys and turned them in Friday, she was hoping to get through the day with few distractions.

Heather arrived at her office early as planned. She poured her coffee as she thought about how she was going to get everything she had to do done in time for her dinner date with Omar. She needed to stop at the nail shop on the way home, which meant she was going to lose an hour. Feeling upbeat, she went to retrieve her mail from the office.

"Happy Monday." She smiled as Sister Shell, obviously startled, dropped the stack of files she was toting to her desk. Heather immediately noticed that the surveys that she spent all day Friday completing were still in Sister Nena's basket.

Heather looked inquisitively at Sister Shell.

Catching her glance, the sister smiled shyly. "She didn't get them before she left Friday, and she won't be back until Wednesday." She removed the surveys from the basket. "I'll put them up so she won't forget to look at them when she gets back in the office."

Heather stared at her in disbelief.

The thought that she could have completed the work over the weekend and that Sister Nena purposely removed her from her class Friday to prove a point wasn't lost on her.

Heather turned on her heel without letting Sister Shell see how completely outraged she was. *I got two days without that witch,* she thought.

Looking over her calendar, Heather noted that the girls had two small performances left before their grand finale, which wasn't scheduled until the last weekend of May.

She picked up the phone and dialed Saint Paul Academy, and it didn't take long before she heard Mr. Goodman's voice on the other end.

"Mr. Goodman? This is Heather Ford from Fellowship Academy."

"Ms. Ford, what brings me this pleasure?" Chavell was happy to hear from Heather. He and the boys were greatly saddened when they heard about the unfortunate accident. In her absence, Fellowship combined the theater department with the fine arts to make sure the students were ready for the performance. Ms. Ford had prepared the boys well before her ordeal, and the accident only made them determined to show everyone what they learned and to make her proud.

"I'm calling to check on the boys," Heather said.

Chavell took a deep breath. "That would be Jayden, Marcos, and Antonio." He knew how much time she had invested in the boys and hated to disappoint her.

"Yes, I would like them to participate in our summer closing performance." Heather heard the hesitation in his voice. "This is not a pressing matter, Mr. Goodman, you can call me back later this week."

"No. It's fine. I imagine with all the things going on over there you haven't heard about the changes we've had on this end."

"No, I've been out of the loop awhile, Mr. Goodman?" Heather hardly ever read the newspaper and got most of the current news from her mother. She couldn't remember her mother mentioning anything about changes in the schools.

"They are cutting the budget again, and sadly, it hit us directly. The school decided it would be a better use of funds to stagger the boys' entrance into our program over the course of two years instead of starting them all together. This will allow the vetting process to be more thorough."

"What do you mean stagger the entrance over two years?" Heather couldn't believe what she was hearing. "That makes no sense. How are they going to decide who starts the program first . . . and won't the boys be entering their junior year?"

"I know, Ms. Ford, I have the same concerns. I have spoken with the boys and their parents and didn't get a good response." Chavell could hear the hurt in Heather's tone and knew she cared deeply for the boys.

Heather was exasperated. "How in the world will they even benefit from the program if they don't enter until their junior year?"

"You're right, Ms. Ford, so the biggest thing for now is keeping them interested in our programs until we can get them in here." Chavell had many of the same concerns as Heather and was the loudest voice in opposition to the new proposal.

"So will you continue working with them through your mentoring program?"

"I am putting a plan together now that I will present to the board next week."

"But why do you have to go before the board? If they are stressing over the funds, you know they are not going to approve a two-year mentoring program." Heather didn't hide her dismay.

"You're right, Ms. Ford, resources are limited, but I have to try. By the way, you may want to keep your ear to the ground because I'm hearing that the cuts are going to affect Fellowship as well. I know that meetings are going on all this week with city officials, the board of education, and private organizations. They are discussing how to give grant money and private funds to privately funded schools in return for programs such as the one we did with the boys to try to temporarily alleviate some of the pressure off the public schools while they go through the process of implementing charter schools."

So that's where Sister Nena is, Heather thought.

"Mr. Goodman, go ahead and write us into the mentoring process for the boys. I can continue to work with them in our theater department, which may help to keep them motivated."

"I really appreciate it." Chavell was elated by the unexpected support from Heather. "With Fellowship backing the mentoring program, I have a stronger case when I go before the board."

"I will talk with Sister Nena about it when she returns, but it shouldn't be a problem." Heather was glad she called. So much had happened in her absence, but now she had a renewed purpose.

~

As she went through her day, she took note of all the areas she could use the boys in. As the girls practiced their new parts, she started to see gaps in the production that could be filled with Jayden's humor. She even started working on small skits for Marcos and Antonio while putting together a list of much-needed props that the boys could build over the summer.

As the day progressed, Heather's excitement grew, and her list of things to do got longer. She found herself rummaging through the storage room, which was stacked to the ceiling with boxes filled with old costumes and fabrics, chairs, and damaged props from years of shows in the old theater. The dust was overwhelming, and she added "cleaning out storage room" to her list of things the boys could do. She saw some old wood pushed precariously against the back wall, which she made several unsuccessful attempts to pull closer to the door. The tiredness in her back and legs brought her to reality. She looked at her watch, which, to her dismay, showed three forty-five.

She pressed her way out of the dust and grime to get to her office. She had lost track of the time. Her goal was to leave thirty minutes early to get to the nail shop, but she was leaving fifteen minutes late.

~

When Omar walked in the office that morning, his secretary and partners were assembling in the conference room. He had no idea what was going on until his secretary put the message in his hand. All the thoughts that went through his head at that moment caused him to become dizzy. The message was from a D&D representative canceling their meeting scheduled for the end of the month due to a conflict with scheduling. The message stated that the only time the board had open until the end of June would be today at ten o'clock. The buzz in the office was electric with everyone talking at once, trying to decide if they should postpone or push to close the heavy contract in two hours.

Omar dialed Lana's number. *She really came through*, he thought as the ringing stopped and her voice mail picked up the call. He wanted to chat with her first to make sure this was her setup. He turned to his secretary. "Call them and tell them we'll be there."

The room got quiet fast.

"Omar, are you sure you want to move on this right now?" Voices on the right. "We could use this next month to gather more data, but if you screw this up today, we'll never get back in to meet with these guys." Coming from the left.

Omar did everything he could to reassure the partners, who were obviously shaken, but in the end, he had to make a decision. He and his assistant gathered the data and materials from the team and prepared for the forty-five-minute drive ahead alone.

He didn't know what to expect. He hadn't looked at any of the company data in weeks. He hadn't been briefed by the team on this company in weeks, so he wasn't sure what was on the PowerPoint that they had updated. His heart was pounding, and the closer he got to Detroit, the more he felt like throwing up. He couldn't believe he was relying on Lana, a woman he just met, to come through for him. What if she had nothing to do with this meeting and this was just as the message said, a scheduling conflict.

He dialed Lana's number again. Again no answer.

"Open that binder and read me the synopsis on the first page, the company overview, find the proposal, and get our recommendations out." Omar barked the orders, and Terry, his personal assistant, immediately searched for the requested documents. He worked with Omar for a while and knew how he got before a major meeting.

Omar listened as Terry read the requested documents out loud for the duration of the ride. When they pulled into the parking garage, his heart was pounding deep and hard in his chest as he struggled to retain the information that Terry was obediently providing.

He called Lana again, and yet again, no answer.

There was nothing left to do other than go in and make the sell. He was not a praying man, but as they walked across the parking lot, he quoted his mom's favorite prayer, "Lord, make a way out of no way. Amen."

They arrived twenty minutes early, which gave Omar a few minutes to glance over the slides that would be presented in the presentation.

"Mr. Eden, follow me, please."

Omar developed tunnel vision as he and Terry followed the secretary down the long foyer. He was grateful for Terry, who didn't miss a beat. Immediately upon entering the room, he began setting up the technology. The room was massive, and in the center was a table that seated at least twenty, and over half of the chairs were occupied. Omar immediately prepared for battle.

He shook several hands before finally meeting the owner and CEO of the company. He was surprised that David was a young man in his early forties. He had an easy smile, and when they shook hands, Omar felt like he was meeting an old friend.

"Okay, everyone, let's get started." David waited for everyone to take their seats. "I'm glad that Mr. Eden responded at such late notice to this meeting."

Omar sat down and prepared for his introduction. "In the files before you are the financial reports from the first-quarter and second-quarter projections."

Everyone began looking through the documents in front of them. Omar glanced at the projections and decided to note them when he gave his presentation. He was able to relax as the board went over the budget, which lasted about forty minutes.

"Turn to page 10 and you will see the overview of United Investors Associations, we are impressed with this company's success record. UIA has been patiently awaiting a response to this proposal that has been sitting on my desk for two months." He paused briefly as everyone looked over the proposal.

"We will vote on this matter after lunch. Mr. Eden, would you like to add anything?"

After glancing through the package presented to the board, Omar saw that they had his entire presentation already; someone from the office had sent them the updated data report and the PowerPoint. He decided against going over everything as planned.

He stood and began reflecting briefly on their budget concerns for the next quarter. He explained how UIA would work with them to relieve the pressure of quarterly budget adjustments by strengthening the company's portfolio and building the wealth within the company. He ended by saying that UIA has been around a long time with proven success. When Omar sat down, he only heard silence. No smiles. No one looked in his direction. Everyone was looking at the PowerPoint and documents in front of them.

Mr. Baine broke the silence. "Okay, you have a working lunch. Return at one o'clock to vote on this proposal."

Omar's mouth went dry as everyone gathered their things and filed out of the room. He turned as Mr. Baine approached him. "Good job, Mr. Eden, enjoy your lunch. My secretary will be in contact with you soon." He shook his hand firmly and turned and walked away.

"What just happened?" Omar whispered to Terry as they followed the crowd out of the building.

~

Lunch was impossible. Omar had so many questions going through his mind that he couldn't taste his food. He was so proud of the team he put together to tackle this giant and said just that repeatedly while Terry responded each time by nodding his head. He realized he was rambling nonstop as his nerves got the best of him, and he finally pushed his food away.

When the phone finally rang, Omar answered it, not realizing that he was holding his breath until he heard Mr. Baine's voice saying, "Mr. Eden, welcome to the team. I am looking forward to working with your firm. Don't let me down."

Omar listened in silent disbelief as Mr. Baine provided the names of his direct contacts and transferred him over to the receptionist to schedule upcoming appointments.

Finally! Omar thought as he walked from the restaurant with his newest client on the line. His team had done their job. He stood grinning from ear to ear. He had finally closed his first multimillion-dollar deal.

Chapter Thirteen

It was after five when Heather got on the highway headed Omar's way. She rushed everything trying to get there on time. She called before she left but was sent to his voice mail. So she sent a text.

"Leaving out—running late. Will be a little after six."

She was finally able to relax as she sat back and listened to Mary J. singing her heart out. As she drove past the field where she had her accident, she tried to see if the tire tracks were still there, but the grass had grown up and covered any sign of the accident. She followed the GPS through two counties and found herself in a hilly area with beautiful homes amid rolling trees. According to the GPS, she was expecting to arrive at her destination in a quarter of a mile. So Heather immediately pulled down the mirror to touch up her makeup.

"Your destination is on the right," the female voice announced from the GPS. Heather turned into the drive of a beautiful brick home. The U-shaped drive was filled with cars, and more cars were parking in the grass and along the street. Heather was certain she was at the wrong place, but the house number, 301, was right in front of her. She immediately called Omar. He answered on the second ring, but before he could speak, the loud music came screaming through the phone, and Heather knew she was at the right place.

"Uh, Omar?" Heather was not sure what was going on, but she had no intention of meeting a lot of people that she didn't know. She immediately started looking for a way to back out the driveway but found she was trapped between a BMW and a Lexus. "What is going on?" she asked cautiously, realizing she had no way to escape.

"Something *big!* Are you here?" Omar rushed to the porch to see Heather standing in the driveway. He ran toward her, and she braced herself as he grabbed her in the heaviest bear hug she ever experienced. When she finally pulled herself from his arms, she saw immediately that he had been drinking—heavily.

Heather felt uncomfortable by Omar's forwardness. "Omar, I'm not sure what's going on, but think I need to leave." Heather was feeling more nervous by the minute.

"*No!*" Omar yelled dramatically. "I want you here."

"I did it! Well, we did it!" He was spinning her around in circles. She couldn't help the smile that started to spread across her face. Most men didn't let all their emotions show, but Omar didn't mind letting it all hang out—joy, sadness, or compassion. He was the most sincere person she had ever met.

"What did *we* do?" Heather yelled, hoping to share his excitement.

"*We* just signed a multimillion-dollar contract with Dukes & Duchess." Omar became extremely still as he watched every emotion he had been feeling all day roll across Heather's face. Excitement finally registered as she realized how major this was for him.

Did he say a multimillion dollar contract? Before she knew it, she was jumping up and down, sharing his foolish outpour of emotions.

"I'm sorry, I didn't cook the meal today, but we got food for days," he said breathlessly, grabbing her around her waist and pulling her toward the house.

"Everyone from the office is here," he said as they entered his beautiful home. "Come on in and meet my partners."

Heather was hesitant only for a moment. Omar made her feel like they had known each other for years although it was only two days and some hours. She looked around her and decided to shed her reserve and enjoy herself. Everyone around her was happy. People were dancing and laughing. Omar was so excited he talked all evening, pulling her from one person to the other, introducing her to everyone as his close friend. At some point, Heather forgot about the newness of their relationship and completely relaxed. She laughed and talked to his partners and coworkers as if they were old friends. Before long, she found her way to the kitchen where she prepared plates for the guest. One of the ladies from the office approached her to tell her that the washroom was out of tissue. Heather apologized and went into the pantry, grabbed a few rolls, and restocked each bathroom.

She felt like she was in one of her dreams, but for the first time, she didn't want to wake up. She went into Omar's bedroom and called Cheri to tell them everything that was going on. She had to talk as fast as she could because she didn't want anyone to miss her absence from the party.

Cheri was so happy for Heather. "What are the chances that the guy that you so happen to meet twice for the first time will be a millionaire?" she said in total disbelief. "He's obviously into you, Heather."

"You think so?" Heather couldn't stop smiling.

"Positive. He wouldn't be parading you around his colleagues if he wasn't. Be careful, though, because sweetness draws roaches, watch how many come out when the word gets out about this contract. Believe me, they're coming."

Heather eased her way back into the full but thinning crowd just as Omar came into the house. "Where you been, baby? I've been looking for you." When Omar embraced her as they stood in the middle of the living room and kissed her on her forehead, time stood still. Heather watched the expressions on every face around them as if in slow motion, and she only saw joyous approval from everyone. It was in that moment that her heart melted, and she allowed herself to be swept away.

"Aye, Maree!" someone yelled from the front of the house, breaking the trance. Omar immediately turned as his best friend walked up and greeted him. "Man, I just heard—" Stephon stopped midsentence, looking at Heather curiously until Omar turned and pulled her close to him.

"Maree, you're holding back? Aren't you going to introduce us?"

Omar looked at Stephon, unsure what atrocities would come out of his mouth.

"Hi, I'm Heather, a friend of Omar, and you are?" Heather had been introducing herself to Omar's friends all day, so she had no qualms when Stephon came up.

"I am Stephon the Great," Stephon said jokingly. "Very nice to meet you, Heather, and if you have any problems with Maree here"—Stephon grabbed Omar playfully—"just call me, and I'll take care of him for you." Stephon slapped Omar in the back before heading to the kitchen to get a beer.

"Mary?" Heather said as soon as Stephon was out of earshot. "Your nickname is Mary?"

Omar laughed. "Mah-ree, not Mary, most of the guys I grew up with still call me that from way back in the day." He smiled down at Heather, glad she was sharing this moment with him.

Heather stood in Omar's embraced, knowing that this was her moment, and decided to change her ringtone to Nicki Minaj's "Moment 4 Life" as soon as she got a chance.

"It's almost eleven. Call in and tell them you won't be in tomorrow." Omar didn't want Heather to leave. "I owe you dinner, remember?" Heather smiled and attempted to kiss him on his lips, but her kiss landed on his chin, causing him to chuckle. "Oh, I must be slipping if that's all I get."

Heather was embarrassed that her first kiss was a near miss. "I'm going to call in," she said, starting to feel the effect from the alcohol and atmosphere.

The hours passed, and Heather was surprised at the number of people that stayed through the night. They sat up and talked until well after two, until Omar got up to go to the bathroom and never returned. Heather found him passed out across his bed. She didn't think twice about crawling next to him and falling asleep.

~

Heather sat on the porch balcony that seemed to be floating midair above the trees, sloping down the side of the mountain. She sat in awe, peering at the rooftops of the huge homes below. How beautiful and peaceful it is up here, she thought, looking down at the marble floor. Mom and Dad can't possibly afford this place. She rubbed her hand along the exquisite trimming of the door. I'm going to start sending them something each month to help with the bills.

The realization of her dad's passing a few years early faded quickly as she heard his voice coming from the sitting room inside.

Heather walked inside and noticed several people sitting around, talking with her mother and father. She didn't recognize anyone except her uncle and aunt sitting on the far side of the room. Heather couldn't find a seat, so she stood casually against the wall. Her uncle looked around the house in amazement. He leaned over and whispered to her aunt that he wanted to build one just like it. (Heather was surprised because her aunt and uncle had just bought a new house and had just recently finished furnishing it.) There was a pile of rocks in front of them at their feet. (Heather recognized the biggest one to be from a centerpiece at her house.) Her uncle casually sorted through the rocks, choosing the ones that he thought would be best for the foundation of the new house he was planning to build.

Heather went in the bedroom to lie down but found that she couldn't rest. She decided it was time to head home. Walking through the living room, she noticed her uncle picking other rocks for his house. One of the rocks he chose was a fossilized rock given to her by one of her students. She stopped to tell him that she wanted to keep the rock but changed her mind as she walked out the door.

Heather boarded a bus that sped down the mountain on tight narrow roads. When they arrived in the city, Heather decided to get off at a coffee shop where she sat for hours, staring out the window. Instead of catching the bus home, she walked several blocks up the street and crossed a huge parking lot with a partial wire fence that had collapsed on one side. Several guys were standing around smoking cigarettes as she approached, but she wasn't afraid. Everything seemed unfamiliar as she approached three doors, not sure which apartment was hers. The third door was wrapped in a big chain and lock, so she stepped to the door in front of her and turned the knob. *This is it,* she thought calmly as the door opened.

She stepped in the room, and immediately, her eyes fell on the glass incubator in the corner of the room. She stood in the door for a moment, looking at the glass cover before realizing something was inside. She stepped closer, cautiously peering through the glass. To her horror, there was a lifeless baby zipped inside some type of plastic bag. Heather snatched the lid of the incubator and saw that moisture and steam made it difficult to see the baby's *face through the bag.* Heather quickly unzipped the bag, and immediately, the baby gasped and took a breath as color flooded back into her tiny face.

Heather's hand shook as she pulled the tiny infant to her chest. *The baby was no more than a week old. Was this her baby?* She reached down and touched her stomach. *Did I have a baby?*

Why didn't I know she was here . . . alone . . . all day. Tears rolled down her face.

Heather felt Omar's arms tighten around her as she fought to snatch out of the grasp of her uncontrollable thoughts. "It's okay," he whispered in her ear, and Heather felt, for the first time in months, untouchable. When he started kissing her, the chemistry between them was undeniable. She felt what he felt and wanted what he wanted. As they undressed each other, there was no resistance. Heather grabbed his hands, and he stopped immediately. "Are you drunk?" she asked, wanting him to remember this moment in the morning.

"No." He leaned forward, fighting the heat that was growing from his groins. "Are you drunk?" he whispered for the same exact reason.

"No." Heather was beyond stopping.

"Good," he said as he took her, knowing there was no looking back.

~

Heather sat up in bed as the memory of the night came flooding back. It was almost lunchtime. She looked around her at Omar's room. It looked like a storm had come through. The lamp and everything from the top of the nightstand was on the floor along with several condom wrappers (what a relief). She stumbled over to pick up the overturned chair and turned to see that the only thing left on the bed was the sheet that she was now dragging behind her as she tripped all the way to the bathroom. As the water from the shower ran down her back, Heather felt more alive than the day she was born. She wanted to be close to him. She wondered what he was doing as she grabbed one of his shirts from his closet. Not sure if guests were still there, Heather pulled her pants on and went to the kitchen.

True to his word, Omar was preparing her lunch. When Heather entered the kitchen, he handed her a glass of wine.

"Surprised?" he said as he walked over and kissed her dead smack on the forehead.

"I must be slipping if that's all I get," Heather said, wrapping her arms around his neck and planting the sexiest good-morning kiss she could muster on his lips.

"Oh my," Omar said jokingly, "if you want me to finish this gourmet meal, then you might want to go way over there."

Heather laughed and took her place at the table. "What do we have here?"

"Well," Omar said, presenting Heather with each portion, "you have a spinach salad with a light raspberry vinaigrette and pecans. You don't have peanut allergies do you?"

Heather giggled. "Nope. No peanut allergies."

He didn't miss a beat. "Good, with blackened shrimp . . . and white wine . . . followed by baked salmon with a golden glaze sauce and lemon."

Heather was more than impressed.

"Go ahead, taste it." Omar stood back and waited as Heather tasted a bit of each dish. He was grinning from ear to ear. "Ain't it good?" He didn't need her to tell him. This was his favorite dish to prepare, and he had cooked it so much he had pretty much perfected it.

Heather nodded. "It's so unbelievably good!"

"I'm not finished." Omar turned and placed a fried biscuit battered in sugar with strawberry and whipped cream on top. "Your dessert."

"Oh my god! Omar, that looks sooo good." Heather stuck her fork in the dessert and was not disappointed as the flavor exploded in her mouth. "It tastes like glory."

He stood for a moment, proudly watching as she savored each bite.

When they finished eating, Heather volunteered to clean up the kitchen as Omar excused himself to make a call to the office. Omar knew his team was working hard to satisfy their new client. After calling, he found that everything was going as planned. As an afterthought, he dialed Lana's number and was surprised when she actually answered the phone.

"Omar? I thought you forgot about me," Lana said coyly.

"No, baby, I haven't forgotten about you. I called you several times yesterday and couldn't get through. It's you who forgot about me." Omar sat down on the bed, trying to get his thoughts together.

"Come on now, Omar, I would never forget about you. Did David call you?" she asked, knowing full well that he had. She and David spoke regularly. He and her sister married right after high school while she was still in grade school. They were married for fourteen years before her sister lost her battle with breast cancer. David has been there for her as a mentor and best friend all her adult life.

"Did he call? Yes, he called! We met and signed the contract yesterday! How did you manage to pull that off?"

"That's my secret." Lana smiled. "Guess what? I'm headed your way. It's time to celebrate!"

Omar jumped from the bed. "Headed this way?" He was not sure if he heard her correctly.

"Yes, I have a few more errands, but they will only take a minute."

Omar's mind was racing.

"Lana, now is not a good time. I had the whole office over last night, and a few people are still here . . . The house is a mess."

"You had your entire office over to celebrate and you didn't invite me?" Lana said, pouting.

"No, it's not like that, Lana. I tried calling you several times but couldn't get through. Right now is not a good time."

Lana couldn't believe Omar was really putting her off. "Are you saying that I can't celebrate with your colleagues?"

"No, it's nothing like that. It's just not a good time," Omar said, all the while knowing that Lana was not the type to take no for an answer. Especially not after she had done so much for him.

There was a long pause, and Omar knew she was pissed. "Give me a couple of hours, and I will call you . . ." The silence on the other end was the first indicator.

"Hello? Hello?" He said the words, but he already knew. She had hung up.

Omar's heart flopped in his chest. He felt it in the pit of his stomach; she was coming.

Chapter Fourteen

Having spent Saturday night with Lana, he didn't want her to think of him as a womanizer. He definitely didn't want her to think he didn't appreciate her helping him close the biggest contract of his career. He did something that he rarely did. He panicked.

Omar grabbed Heather's purse from the dresser and went into the living room.

Heather had just finished cleaning the kitchen and was about to start with the rest of the house when he rushed into the living room. "What's wrong?" she asked as he sat her purse on the couch.

"I have an emergency at work, and I'm going to have to head out," he said matter-of-factly, hoping Heather would hear the intensity in his voice. She didn't. She continued picking up trash off the coffee table. He grabbed the plastic bag from her hand, refusing to look her in the face.

"Baby, go ahead and get dressed. I'm going to have to leave in about ten minutes." He needed time to figure out how to handle Lana. He definitely didn't want Heather to be here when she got here; Lana could ruin him.

Heather was disappointed by the abrupt end of the day, but hearing that there was something wrong and seeing the sudden change in Omar's demeanor made her go ahead and start grabbing her things that were scattered around the house. She could only imagine what could have gone wrong. His life was so different from hers. Her problems with Sister

Nena seemed minute compared to managing finances of multimillion-dollar companies. She got her purse and waited for him to get dressed. Omar grabbed the first thing his hands touched, which ended up being some sweatpants and a Nike shirt. Heather watched as he put on the sports attire. She never saw him dressed so casual and was surprised that he was going to work in sport attire.

Heather was determined not to slow his progress as she watched him hurrying around the house. Since they were taking the same highway out, she decided to go outside and wait for him.

Omar was relieved when Heather walked out to the porch and quickly went behind her to say good-bye. It wasn't until he got outside that he realized she was waiting for him to get in his car so they could leave together. Flabbergasted, he wasn't sure how he was going to get her to leave without him actually driving off with her.

"I forgot my keys," he said, patting his pockets blindly before running back into the house. As he ran back in the house, Heather decided to go ahead and leave so he could focus on getting to the office. Before she could get the words out, she heard a car pull into the driveway.

Omar's heart fell to his feet as he stepped onto the porch with his keys in his hand and the cream Coupe whipped into the driveway.

Lana pulled to a stop right in front of the porch. Heather watched as the young white girl stepped from the car. She ran up the stairs, greeting Heather with a nod as she grabbed Omar and kissed him long and hard on the mouth.

"Aww, is everyone leaving?" she asked as she peeped inside the house.

When she saw the mess left from the night before, she was surprised. "It really *is* a mess!" she said, surprised that he was telling the truth. Lana recognized Heather immediately from the café Saturday. *She must be a new client*, she thought, turning to Heather, and apologetically said, "I told him that he didn't have to get rid of everyone on my account. I'm sorry I missed the celebration party yesterday." She pouted and looked at Omar seductively. "That's okay, we'll have our own celebration." Omar stood in the doorway as Lana brushed past him and entered the house.

Heather stared at him in total shock. "So this is the emergency at the office?" she said, trying to take everything in. "You were doing all this to get me out of your house."

Omar did anything he could to keep from looking at Heather. "No, Heather, it's not what you think." He didn't know what to say. "I wish I could explain, but it's so . . . complicated."

"Complicated! What do you mean *complicated?*"

Heather was getting louder, and he didn't want Lana to hear their conversation.

"Heather, I have so much going on right now." How could he explain what he was still trying to figure out himself? "I swear this wasn't supposed to happen." He wanted to tell her that he cared about her, but he knew it wouldn't matter at this point. He had so much riding on Lana right now that he couldn't lose her. "I just need you to leave right now, and I promise I will call you later, and we can discuss everything."

"Why would you do this to me?" Her eyes searched his, looking for the spark that was there during lunch, but Omar refused to meet her gaze; the hurt in her eyes crushed him. "What was all this about? For sex?" Heather felt her eyes starting to water, but her pride would not let him see how much hurt she felt. She turned and walked quickly down the steps, expecting to hear something from him, but when she got to her car, she turned and saw that he was gone.

~

Thick tears flooded her eyes, blinding her as she tried to get as far away from any memory of Omar as fast as she could.

"I can't believe I fell for this stupid fairy tale crap," she said as the realization that she was talking to herself like a crazy person made her more upset. *"Did I misread the signals?"*

Heather wondered if Omar was faking the whole time.

If he knew he had someone, why would he introduce me to all his coworkers?

He introduced her to everyone as a "good friend." What is a *good friend?*

Absolutely nothing.

"What was I thinking?"

Heather couldn't believe she fell so hard for this guy. And to add insult to injury, he was drunk every time they were together. If any of her friends told her that they were dating a drunk, she would tell them to drop him. So what if he's cute or has money?

Why didn't they warn me? It was obvious that Mah-ree, Mary, or whatever his friends called him, had a drinking problem.

What kind of nickname is Maury anyway?

It was at that moment that she remembered the late-night call. Someone called her saying he was an old friend of hers; his name was Maury.

It couldn't be . . . was it?

It was him!

He set her up.

Her hands began shaking uncontrollably. Just knowing that he knew who she was and had lied about everything was terrifying.

Why would someone do this to her? She struggled to swallow as her mouth went dry.

He was a creep.

She looked at the speedometer and saw that she was going forty miles per hour in a six-five zone. She could not get her muscles in her legs to move to press the accelerator. Heather struggled to catch her breath as she felt the pain of betrayal stab like a knife in her chest.

She was having trouble breathing, and her hands were shaking so bad that she could barely grip the steering wheel.

She could hear her heart beating in her ears, a deafening sound that, along with her failed attempts to get air to her lungs, was putting her in a trance. She looked out the window at the trees on both sides of the road, but fear wouldn't allow her to pull over. As the early signs of panic overwhelmed her, she tried her best to focus on something else, but the pain in her chest was debilitating. She was not going to make it home.

Heather pressed the call button on the steering wheel.

"Who would you like to call?"

"Call Ellis."

Heather's voice was barely audible, and she was relieved to hear the call going through.

"Calling Ellis."

Ellis, where are you? Heather was pleading as the ringing continued, unanswered.

Chapter Fifteen

Ellis was lying on the couch asleep when he felt someone shaking to wake him. It took him a moment to realize Lisa was standing over him with his work phone vibrating furiously in her hand.

"Baby, wake up!" Lisa hated to wake him. He had worked four straight days, and she knew he was exhausted. "It was the hospital," she said as the ringing stopped.

Ellis's eyes flew open, and he grabbed the phone from his wife's hand. He glanced quickly at the name that appeared across the screen, ER-4.

The hospital-issued phone was his direct line to the emergency call center, but when Heather was in the hospital, he saved Mrs. Ford's number in the contact as ER-5. He had Heather's house, cell, and car saved under different numbers, ER-2 through ER-4. He did this just in case he misplaced the phone and it was returned to the hospital. He really didn't want anyone, not to mention his wife, knowing the names of the patients he kept in contact with.

"Where's my notebook?" he asked Lisa, pretending to look for something that wasn't there. She went into the kitchen to see if his logbook was on the counter. He jumped off the couch quickly and ran upstairs. Out of earshot of his wife, he dialed Heather's number.

"I hear you're cheating on me," he said as soon as he heard her pick up the phone.

Heather was relieved to hear Ellis's voice coming loudly through her speakers. She felt laughter in her chest, but the tears rolled instead. She was out of breath and losing focus.

There was a long pause on the line.

"Heather? What's wrong? Heather, are you okay?" he asked but only heard Heather crying on the other end.

"Are you driving?"

"Heather, where are you?" Ellis was beginning to panic. "Heather, I need you to talk to me, baby. Tell me what's going on." The deafening silence unnerved him as he muted the phone and ran down the stairs.

"I'm sorry, baby, I got to get to the hospital," he said, tripping over the blanket and shoes that were lying on the floor. He reached for his jeans that were on the back of the couch, checking for his wallet and keys as Lisa handed him his logbook.

"Found it in the bathroom on the back of the toilet." She smiled, shaking her head.

"How did it get in there?" Ellis said sarcastically, quickly pulling her into his arms. "I hate leaving you like this," he said, rubbing the side of her stomach, "but duty calls."

Lisa smiled playfully. "Okay, I'm going to see if you're rubbing on this in a couple of months," she said, touching her belly that was surprisingly flat even though she was thirteen weeks pregnant.

"Oh, I will," he said, rushing out the door.

"Heather? Are you there?" Ellis started the car and backed out of the driveway.

"I'm driving," Heather managed to get the words out in a whisper. "I'm scared." Her eyes were burning from the sweat that covered her face.

"Press the OnStar button, I'm on my way. Heather? Press the button!" Ellis was yelling out of frustration.

Heather pushed the button.

"OnStar, what's your emergency?"

"This is Ellis Saxton, Am-Stat driver 54. My friend has called me with an emergency. Can you tell me the location of this vehicle so I can assist?"

"Driver 54, this is Jena. Aren't you off this weekend?" Jena said, recognizing Ellis's voice immediately.

"Yes, I am, but I will take this call. If further assistance is needed, I will call dispatch. I need the location, please."

"Highway 82 north of Count Road 37. Southbound thirteen miles from Morgan County."

"Okay. Thank you. I'm in route."

"Heather, I need you to pull over," Ellis spoke as calmly as he could.

"I can't, somebody could be out there." Heather could hardly recognize her voice. Her body was visibly trembling as she gripped the wheel with both hands.

Heather flinched as a big rig passed her. She couldn't blame the driver. She was going thirty-five miles per hour.

"Where are you?" she whispered, hoping Ellis could hear her.

"I'm coming, but I need you to get off the road."

Ellis pleaded with her for fifteen minutes trying to get her to focus, but she wasn't listening.

"Okay, I see you ahead of me. Pull over." Ellis said sternly. He was traveling between eighty and ninety miles per hour and rolled up on her pretty quick.

Heather pulled her car over into the gravel and unlocked the door.

Ellis jumped from the car and ran to her door. He opened the door slowly, not sure what to expect. He could see Heather was drenched in sweat. Her hair was wet and sticking to her forehead. Her eyes were dark and running with mascara and tears.

"You look a mess," he said as he pulled her from behind the wheel.

The cool air helped as Ellis leaned up against the side of the car and held Heather in his arms as she struggled to regulate her breathing and maintain her balance.

Heather laid her head against Ellis's chest. She felt exhausted. "Do I really look a mess?" she said through tears.

Ellis looked at Heather, knowing that she if knew how attractive she was to him, she wouldn't ask. "Yep," he said, smiling down at her.

"Shut up," Heather said playfully as she pulled away from him.

"I feel so stupid, Ellis." Heather could feel the tears welling again. Heather took slow deep breaths, trying to compose herself. "Mama was right." She laughed through her pain. She looked up and saw Ellis looking at her. "She was right." Acute embarrassment embraced her as she thought of Ellis's commitment to her recovery. He is the rock for her, and her mother and she completely ignored him. She disregarded him when he has been a part of her life, but chased a man who she didn't know anything about and who didn't care about her. Heather could not stop the overwhelming sense of sadness at that moment. She put her head down and cried. Ellis wrapped his arms around her, astounded by her raw emotions.

"I'm sorry to keep bothering you, Ellis." Between her and her mother, she was sure Ellis never thought he would meet such needy women.

His embrace calmed her. "What took you so long to get here?" she said jokingly in an effort to get her mind off the fact that they were standing on the side of the road. Her mother was right. Why was she looking for a good man when Ellis was right here.

"What do you mean? I jumped in my jet and flew thirty-five miles in eleven minutes. I didn't have any problem finding you because you were speeding up the road, going thirty-two miles per hour in a sixty-five zone," Ellis said, pleased to see her smiling through her tears. "Where are you coming from anyway?"

"From nowhere." Heather opened the door and sat down in her car. "I'm coming from absolutely nowhere."

Chapter Sixteen

H eather made it to work an hour early.
She found that lying in bed only brought haunting dreams, and sitting idle brought unwanted images. She had no escape. Her plan was to dive as deep as she could into her work, and since Sister Nena was returning to work today, Heather decided that she would be satisfied with making it through the day without dealing with her negativity.

She sat at her desk, struggling to focus on the script in front of her, and reluctantly picked up the phone and called Cheri.

"Girl, I been thinking about you all night." Cheri answered the phone on the second ring.

She and Janet had been talking about Heather for the last two days, and she couldn't wait to get the latest gossip. "Okay, I'm ready," she said, sitting up in her bed. "Don't leave anything out."

Heather didn't know where to start but decided that it didn't matter where she started. The end would always be the same.

"His girlfriend showed up," Heather said bluntly.

"*Girlfriend!*" Cheri's reaction was just as expected. "Hold up, what do you mean *his girlfriend* showed up? Why would he have you *at his house* if he had a girlfriend?"

"Don't know, but yep. She showed up." Cheri's anger made Heather feel a little better.

"What did she say?" Cheri couldn't believe what she was hearing. "What did you do?" Cheri walked over to her morning bar and poured a glass of wine. "When did this happen? Why didn't you call?"

"Everything happened Tuesday. We were together all day Monday, just like I told you. He convinced me to take off yesterday so we could spend some private time together." Heather paused as the memories invaded her thoughts. "I stayed." She sighed loudly, trying to prepare herself before recounting the horrid events. "Tuesday he fixed me this delicious lunch with salad, salmon, wine, a delicious dessert, and . . . he went to make a phone call . . . came back saying he had an emergency at work and I had to go . . . was pretty much trying to push me out the house, but before I got out . . . she pulled up." Heather wiped the tears from her face.

"Oh, Heather, I am so sorry." Cheri sympathized with her friend. "She must've been out of town or something. What did she say when she saw you?"

"Nothing. She just smiled at me and kissed him before going in the house. Apparently he told her that he had people over from the office and he was getting everyone out so he could clean up because she said something about everyone leaving before she got there."

"Why didn't you say something?" Cheri felt her friend's pain and could hear her sobbing quietly on the other end. "You should've put him on blast because I'm sure she didn't know. At least both of you would have known where you stood with him."

"I know, Cheri. It all happened so fast that I didn't know what to do."

"Well, what did she look like?"

"Very pretty white girl, young, well put together. You can tell she comes from money. That wasn't my first time seeing her though. She was leaving when I met him downtown Saturday, but she was picking up cards like she was getting information about his company."

"Well, if she was meeting him Saturday, what makes you think she's his girlfriend?" Cheri was pissed off. "I'm going to let you get to work, but I think she simply staked her claim like I told you to do. Dude hit the jackpot, and the roaches came running just like I told you."

"It wasn't about her," Heather said through frustration. "I could care less about her staking claim or disrespecting me. I care that when she walked up, Omar looked me in my face, turned, and followed her in the house like a sick, starving puppy. He left me there. He didn't pretend to care, just shrugged and walked away." Heather was tired of talking about it.

"You're right Heather. He's a dog walking on two legs. I thought he would be different. I just wish I was there when that hepher disrespected you. Sweetie, keep your head up. I'll call you later."

It took Heather a minute to take in everything her friend said before she realized that she felt worse after the conversation than she did when she first came in to work. She gathered her notes and headed down to the auditorium.

~

After her second class, Heather gathered a few of her students and started digging for treasures in the workroom. The girls looked for props and costumes that they thought fit with the new scripts. She was able to add several new jobs to her summer work list for boys, which made her feel like she had renewed purpose.

She worked through lunch, and as the afternoon approached, she felt her body becoming weak. On her way to the snack machine, she decided to go ahead and talk to Sister Nena about allowing the boys to participate in the closing summer production.

"Sister, can I speak with you?" she said, eager to get this over with.

"Yes, what can I do for you, Ms. Ford?" Sister Nena stopped writing and motioned to the chair.

Heather closed the door and sat down. "I spoke with Mr. Goodman from Saint Paul earlier this week because I wanted to see if the boys that participated during the Christmas holiday were available to make a guest appearance in our summer program." Heather paused for a reply, but there was none. She cleared her throat. "That was when he notified me that they would not be able to start the boys in the fall as planned, but will stagger their entrance into the program over the next two years. I was deeply concerned that the boys would lose interest over such a long time and would like your permission to allow them to continue to earn community service credits while we provide mentoring for them during the summer months."

Sister Nena stared blankly at Heather for a moment before responding. "Ms. Ford, when you spoke with Mr. Goodman, did you ask him if Saint Paul would be providing mentoring for the boys themselves?"

"I did," Heather said confidently. "He said that he was going to present it to their board, but he would have a stronger case if he could tell them that we were on board when he met with them."

Sister Nena sighed loudly. "I do understand that you want to help, Ms. Ford, but this problem is between the city of Flint and Saint Paul. I really don't want Fellowship to get pulled into something that is actually much larger than three inner city boys. Of course, Mr. Goodman would love to be able to walk in that meeting and tell them that Fellowship is going to carry the weight of babysitting these boys for two years, allowing them time to play with city funds until they get ready to use them for the purpose they were allocated for. I'm sorry, but the answer is no."

Heather was completely taken aback by the unexpected response. She wasn't sure if she had explained her proposal wrong.

"I will bear all the burden, Sister. It won't be on Fellowship. We have so many things that need to be done all over this school. I have been generating a list of things that the theater department need done. Having the extra hands will help out every department on this campus." Heather was pleading her case the best she could.

"Ms. Ford, you are an employee of Fellowship Academy. Everything you do falls on our shoulders. The answer is no. Is there anything else?" Sister Nena returned to her work.

"Can we at least allow the boys to participate in the final show in May?" Heather knew she wasn't the only one in this town who saw the importance of helping these boys.

Sister Nena took her reading glasses off and looked at Heather impatiently. "Ms. Ford, Fellowship is an *all-girls* school. The purpose of the summer program is to highlight the talents of the students and to let our donors know that we deserve every penny that they donate each year to keep the doors of the school open. It makes no sense to bring three boys from the street to parade across the stage. This is a private event. Now please excuse me, I have to get back to work."

~

Heather went to her office and locked the door behind her. She sat at her desk and cried until there were no tears left.

Chapter Seventeen

Sister Nena's response to her request caused Heather to question every decision she had made over the last three years, including accepting the position to work at Fellowship.

She had a chance to work in the public schools, but withdrew her application and applied for a position at Fellowship when she heard of the upcoming budget cuts. When they started cutting programs from the public schools, she didn't give much thought to the students she left behind. She was simply relieved that she hadn't taken the job.

Before, she never considered the students and the fact that they wouldn't be exposed to theater, dance, photography, instrumental music, and all the other programs offered in the private sectors. She didn't think to write any letters on behalf of the students and, frankly, didn't lose much sleep over it. But now she was being slapped in the face by the reality of it all. She had a chance to help, but found herself in a situation where she couldn't help because of things out of her control.

Every day just getting out of the bed was becoming a struggle as Heather sank deep into depression. Knowing that she could be doing more and being stopped because of circumstances was taking a mental toll on her. Instead of growing in her career, she was dying every day, suffocating.

As the months passed, Heather became more and more dissatisfied with everything around her. She tried to focus on the girls but couldn't help feeling like she was wasting her time. Heather couldn't shake the feeling that there was something she should be doing, but didn't know exactly what it was. She felt like an emotional wreck and found herself constantly swallowing back tears.

Heather spent her breaks in her office, trying to stay current about the school budget and hoping she would inadvertently find out about the fate of the boys, but Flint crime updates and the budget crises took over the front page every day. By early May, she was heartbroken when the Flint Board of Education announced they were closing two elementary schools and one middle school in the inner city. Heather finally conceded and sided with the hundreds of others who felt the problems in the community were so deeply rooted that no one person or even a group could change it.

~

As the end of the school year quickly approached, the different departments in the school were readying the students for the summer closing program with hopes to impress the parents and donors. Heather watched as the students and parents came in and out of the school for weeks, getting costumes, instruments, and notes about last-minute changes, and everyone except her was buzzing with excitement.

She sat in her office, doing her end-of-the-day routine when one of her students walked in unannounced.

"Excuse me, Amber. I think you need to go out and reenter the correct way," Heather said calmly.

She could tell by her expression that the young girl was annoyed, but she obediently backed out of the door and tapped lightly to gain permission to enter.

"Excuse me, Ms. Ford," she said quietly, "can I speak with you for a second?"

"What can I do for you?" She motioned for her to sit down, curious to know what was obviously bothering her.

"I was told that you cut my part out of the final skit," Amber said bluntly.

Heather looked at the child sitting in front of her for a brief moment before responding cautiously.

"Yes, Amber. I did cut the last four minutes of the play, which happened to include your part."

Amber burst into tears. "But why did you cut my part? I worked so hard on it!"

"Amber, your part wasn't the only part cut. I cut the entire skit out because we had to make time for the orchestra to set up for the next set," Heather spoke calmly.

"But Miley doesn't even know her part yet, and my mom told me to come and ask you why you cut my part and not hers." Amber's cheeks were crimson red as she prepared herself for a fight.

"Amber, you have participated in every play this year, Miley hasn't. It's taking her longer to get rid of her stage fright, but she'll be fine." Heather was growing tired of the conversation.

"But why'd you cut me and not her?" Amber responded defiantly.

Heather looked at the ninth grader sitting in front of her and prayed for patience. "Amber, let's start with the fact that I don't appreciate your tone. Number 2, Miley's part is needed to close the story line of the play, and yours is not. If your mother has any more questions, have her call me."

Amber stood to leave. "I'll tell her to call you, but she said you won't be here next year anyway, so she might not even worry about it." Amber retorted over her shoulder as she walked out the door.

Heather's first thought was to call her back and scold her about being disrespectful, but instead, she grabbed her things and locked up her office. What Amber said didn't surprise her. She heard rumors circulating through the school about plans to merge theater with one of the other auxiliaries to save money for new technology in the fall.

Heather sat down in her car and felt all her energy drain from her body. She decided a visit to her mother's house would be the best way to get her mind off the storms brewing around her. Although they spoke daily on the phone, she hadn't stopped by in several weeks. She didn't want her mother asking her questions about Omar or stressing her about Ellis, so she stayed away. Every time she spoke with Ellis, he was fussing about her not checking in on her mother. He was right, but she didn't worry about her mom because she knew he was always there.

~

The smell of smothered chicken and rice greeted her as she entered the house. She immediately walked into the kitchen and hugged her mother, who was surprised to see her.

"Mama?" Heather looked around the kitchen at the covered dishes on the stove top: greens, corn bread, and yams. "Are you expecting guests?"

Mrs. Ford nodded as she pushed Heather away from the stove.

"This is my night to host Bible study, and the mothers are coming by," she said, looking closely at Heather. "I didn't know you were stopping by."

Mrs. Ford was aware that Heather had been avoiding her. She would call to check on her but always kept the conversation brief. On Sundays she started riding to church with one of the other sisters because she never knew if Heather was going. Heather would show up to service, but she was always late. She relied heavily on Ellis, who stopped by at least twice a week and kept her informed about Heather.

"It's good you're here. You can stay for Bible study," she said, her eyes never leaving Heather's face.

Heather had no intention of sitting and listening to her mother and her friends talk for an hour. "No, I'll grab something to go. I've had a long day, I just wanted to see you." Heather smiled weakly.

"What are you putting on your face? Your skin looks really clear," her mother said, placing her plate on the table. "If I didn't know any better, I would've asked if you were pregnant." Mrs. Ford never looked back as she walked down the hall to the sitting room.

Heather couldn't believe her mother had just offhandedly made the pregnant comment to her of all people. The fact that she never knew her mother to make the comment without deep consideration first, coupled with the fact that she was hardly ever wrong, caused Heather to lose her appetite. She went down the hall to the bathroom and stared at her reflection in the mirror. Staring back at her were tired eyes, and with them, she had no idea what her mother saw.

Heather left by easing out through the side door before the church mothers could detain her.

She drove home in deep thought; she took her mother's words seriously. What if she was pregnant? She couldn't check her menstrual date because, thanks to the meds, she hadn't had a regular cycle since the accident.

Instead of turning to go home, Heather headed up the main street, knowing full well what she had to do.

~

She sat on her couch with the phone in her hand.

"Hey, girl." Heather was grateful when Janet's voice interrupted the voices in her head.

"Guess what I'm doing," Heather asked.

"Why, what are you doing?"

"I'm sitting on my couch, waiting on the results from a pregnancy test that I purchased this afternoon," Heather replied dryly.

There was a long pause as Janet struggled to find her voice. "Are you serious?" She was dumbfounded. "How late are you?"

"That's the problem. Since the accident, I've only had one cycle that lasted three days, and that was back in January."

"But what made you get it?" Janet was unaware of Heather going out with anyone since her weekend fling back in late January.

"I stopped in on Mom today, and she made this offhanded comment about me looking pregnant." Heather looked at her reflection in the mirror. "And I have gained a few pounds."

Janet let out a sigh of relief. "Heather, do you know how many times your mother says that someone looks pregnant? Plus, your job has you stressed out. Either you're going to gain weight or lose weight."

Everything Janet said made sense, but Heather couldn't ignore the way she had been feeling lately or the fact that she was becoming extremely emotional, constantly fighting back tears over things that shouldn't matter.

"You're right, Janet," Heather said, getting up from the couch. "There's only one way to find out." She walked into the bathroom and looked at the white towel that she purposely covered the white stick with.

"One line means no, and two lines means kill me now," she said jokingly, trying to relieve the tension as she removed the cover from the stick. She held her breath while trying to figure out which side was the test side and which side was the result side.

The seconds ticked away.

"Well! What does it say?" Janet asked impatiently at the lengthy silence on the other end.

Heather sighed deeply. "It says kill me now."

~

Omar loosened his tie, releasing the tension that was resting on his shoulders. They had been in the meeting for over two hours and still hadn't made much progress in determining the direction they wanted to take the company. After signing with D&D, the phones were ringing off the hook, and they were propelled forward through the business media, becoming the fastest-growing marketing company in the United States. They had each grossed over a quarter million dollars in the first two quarters, and with so many competitors, the focus had shifted from securing contracts to keeping contracts.

Omar felt the message indicator vibrating his phone. He knew it was probably Lana confirming their dinner reservation. He was so busy most days that he didn't have time to get out, but he always made time for Lana. He didn't hear from her often, but when he did, he knew he was in for a treat. He couldn't believe his luck the day she told him about her relationship with David Baine, the CEO of D&D. It was her connection that helped them get to where they are now, and for that, he would always be in debt to her.

He left the office and headed over to Gardinas to meet Lana. When he arrived, she was standing in the lobby, talking with a gentleman that he was unfamiliar with. When he approached them, Lana introduced him, and he immediately excused himself by telling her he was going to check on the reservation. He was fully aware of Lana's affairs and private arrangements and decided months ago that the "don't ask, don't tell" policy was best for them. He was only concerned with their arrangement, which consisted of him being available when she needed him and her providing him information on inside trade deals and high-profile clients when he requested it.

He beckoned for the waiter to place his wine order when he was interrupted by his phone ringing. He sighed and, for a brief second, contemplated ignoring the call but decided against it.

"Omar Eden," he mustered an energetic greeting in case it was a potential client calling.

"Hi, Omar, this is Heather Ford."

~

It took everything short of an act from God for Janet and Cheri to convince Heather to call Omar. After the third positive test result, Heather was finally convinced. Not only was she pregnant, but she was close to sixteen weeks pregnant. The memory of the last time she saw him was fresh on her mind when she dialed the number.

"Heather? Hi . . ." Omar was shocked to hear Heather's voice on the other end.

Although it was only a few months ago, it really seemed like a lifetime. He remembered doing everything he could to get to know her. Those two days were the best days of his life. He signed his first big contract, and they celebrated for two days. They had so much fun. He smiled, thinking of her expression when she tasted the dessert he had cooked. Then it all came to an end. He didn't know what to do when Lana showed up. He punked out. If he knew then what he knew now, he would've just told Lana about Heather, but he didn't, and he ended up playing Heather right to her face. The look on her face standing in his driveway still haunts him. For weeks he contemplated calling her to apologize, but he knew she would never forgive him. He told his secretary to send her flowers on Valentine's Day, but canceled them when he thought about how meaningless contacting her would be. At that time, he walked on eggshells around Lana and didn't want to do anything to jeopardize their relationship.

"Heather, it's good hearing from you," he said sincerely while at the same time thinking that she must really hate him.

"Is this a bad time?" Heather said.

"No, no, you're fine." Omar watched as Lana walked toward the table and sat down. "I have a few minutes. What can I do for you?"

Heather had planned to set up a meeting with Omar so they could sit down and discuss this as adults, but after hearing his voice, she knew that the last thing she wanted to do was see him. She decided to get it over with. Who cares what he thought about her?

"When we were together . . ." she began slowly, but after she started her well-rehearsed speech, she regretted even calling. *Maybe I could hang up, pretend this call never happened, and write a letter and put it in the mail*, she thought to herself.

"You know what, Omar? I wish there was an easy way to have this conversation, but there's not," she stated bluntly. "I have something to tell you. I don't want to do it over the phone, but it's kind of important."

Omar had no idea what Heather was talking about, but he was becoming more uncomfortable by the second. He looked at Lana and excused himself from the table. His mind was racing as he walked to the lobby. Was this the call he prayed he would never get? Is she going to tell him she has some kind of incurable disease? She has HIV or something just as bad.

Omar realized Heather wasn't saying anything. "Hello?"

"Yes, I'm here."

"Go ahead, I'm listening." Omar was becoming extremely nervous. He couldn't believe this was happening to him. He remembered that night, waking up with her in his arms. The voice in his head screamed "Get the condoms," but things got so intense that he chose not to listen. He didn't use anything the first time, but he did every time after that. His mind went to the women he had been with since Heather, and the thought that he would have to notify all of them caused his mouth to go dry, and he started sweating profusely.

"Heather, just say what you need to say!" Omar said through clenched teeth.

"I'm pregnant," Heather blurted out the heaviest words of her life.

"What?" He said although he heard her perfectly clear.

His laugh was loud and harsh as relief washed over him. "Did you say *pregnant?*"

Heather was confused by his response. "Excuse me, but forgive me if I don't see the humor in this situation."

"No, you wouldn't," Omar said, his words dripping with sarcasm as Lana appeared. "You'll be surprised how many women have tried to pull this one. The pregnant call is like the trump card"—he laughed again—"and women just love playing it."

"Is everything okay?" Lana asked, but seeing the anger on Omar's face, she turned and went back into the restaurant.

"No, I am not surprised that you have a problem with getting countless women pregnant," Heather hissed. "Are you implying that I made this up to persuade you to be with me?" Heather couldn't believe his nerve. "Newsflash, Omar Eden, I don't want you. Nor do I need you. I didn't call you to try to get with you or ask you for money. I am calling you to notify you that I am pregnant with your child. So laugh at that, you arrogant, egotistical, pompous bastard!"

Omar held the phone to his ear completely speechless as Heather screamed at him before ending the call abruptly. Lana reappeared with her handbag and keys.

"Are you okay?" she said, taking his arm gently and walking toward the door. Omar looked at her, unsure as to why they were leaving. "I canceled our reservation, I didn't think you would enjoy your meal anyway." Lana smiled sadly as they walked to the parking lot.

She was right. Omar had lost his appetite. "I'm going to take a rain check on that nightcap, Lana," Omar said, knowing she had planned to spend the night with him, but he was not in the mood for company tonight. He closed the door as she got into her car, grateful for her nonchalant attitude. She didn't ask about the call, but simply waved before pulling out of the parking lot.

Chapter Eighteen

Heather scanned through the baby magazines that were thrown precariously across the table. After seeing how excited her mother was about having a grandchild, she started to embrace the idea of being pregnant. After her conversation with Omar, she realized that she was probably going to raise the child alone. Ellis was the last person she told. She thought about asking him to be the godfather, but he was so angry with the news of her pregnancy that he cut her short and got off the phone. He hadn't returned any of hers or her mother's calls.

Heather looked around the room at the expecting women sitting and waiting to be called to the back. They were each at different stages of their pregnancy. Two ladies were talking about how difficult the first three months were for them. Heather smiled because, based on her calculations, she was at least sixteen weeks, which means she missed the sickness that comes in the first trimester.

Heather looked at the woman sitting across from her. She had obviously misplaced something as she was searching frantically through her purse. Frustrated, she stood clumsily and walked toward the door. Heather noticed the set of keys in the chair.

"Excuse me, you're leaving your keys?" Heather said as the lady returned to her seat.

"Thank you, I thought I locked them in the car," she said relieved.

"Girl or boy?" Heather asked as the lady eased down in the chair.

"I prayed for a boy, and it's a boy," she said excitedly.

"You don't look like you have too much longer," Heather said, acknowledging her huge bulge.

The lady sighed loudly. "August 5th, and it feels like time is standing still."

"I can imagine." Heather laughed. "At least you're in the home stretch, I'm just getting started."

"Oh, so this your first visit?" the lady asked, rubbing the side of her belly.

Heather nodded. "And I'm really nervous. I don't have cycles, so I had to guess how far along I am. If it wasn't for my mom, I would've been on that show with those women who go to the bathroom and come out with a baby."

"Oh no, I hope not." The lady giggled. "I've seen that show, and I can't see how a woman can go nine months and not feel all this kicking and pushing." She shifted uncomfortably in her chair.

They both laughed.

Heather realized she hadn't introduced herself. "By the way, I'm Heather, Heather Ford."

"Lisa Saxton," Lisa said, rubbing her underbelly. "Well, Heather, you just wait until you start carrying this weight."

"Do you know Ellis Saxton?" Heather asked, thinking *Saxton* was not a common last name. Lisa could be related to Ellis.

"Yes, he's my husband," Lisa said, surprised that Heather knew Ellis. "How do you know Ellis?"

Heather stared blankly at Lisa. They couldn't possibly be talking about the same person. Heather could see that Lisa was waiting for a response.

"The Ellis I know," she said, choosing her words carefully, "drives the EMT for the hospital." Heather said to reassure Lisa that she was not talking about her husband.

"I know, he's been there for years. Do you work at the hospital?" Lisa asked.

Heather felt like she had gotten kicked in the chest and was rendered speechless. She looked at the concerned look on Lisa's face.

"No, I was in an accident last year, and he was one of the drivers that assisted in saving my life."

Heather said, watching the smile spread across Lisa's face.

"I'm not surprised," she said proudly. "People come up to me all the time, telling me how Ellis saved their life. He is so dedicated to his job."

Heather sat in total disbelief as she listened to Lisa go on and on about Ellis. She practically ran to the nurse when she heard her name called.

The nurse greeted her, but the earth-shattering sound of "I know, he's my husband" left her temporarily deaf.

Heather lay on the table as the doctor checked her cervix, and her thoughts were completely removed. The only thing she could think of was that Ellis was married and his wife was in the next room full of baby. She looked around the room to make sure this wasn't a nightmare as the doctor placed the cold gel on her belly for the ultrasound. The first sound of the tiny heartbeat made her jump.

Ellis is married, she repeated to herself.

The doctor showed her the baby's fully developed body and told her to expect a baby boy on November 6th.

She let the tears fall as she listened to the doctor. There was no way she could knowingly disguise the hurt she felt from this painful betrayal, but the doctor patted her hand and handed her a Kleenex, mistaking her tears for those of joy.

Chapter Nineteen

~Four Years Later~

The sound of glass shattering jerked Heather from a dreamless sleep. As she stood in the doorway of her bedroom, she looked down the hall and saw a large shadow move across the hallway. She knew someone was there. She moved slowly with her back against the wall to Harley's room. He was asleep in his bed. She scooped him up with his blanket wrapped around him and covered his mouth with her hand so he couldn't make a sound. Her heart was racing as they moved quickly to the front door, never taking her eyes off the back bathroom where she believed the intruder to be hiding. Harley began squirming, trying to get out of her arms, and she struggled to get the bolt unlocked on the door. She stepped into the crisp December night and ran quickly down the front steps and to the sidewalk where her neighbors were getting in their car.

When Travis saw Heather running toward him, he knew something was wrong. His wife, Evelyn, immediately jumped from the car.

"Someone is in my house. I think they came in through the back door because I heard when the window broke," she was rambling frantically.

"Are you sure?" Travis said, taking out his phone and dialing 911.

"Yes, I saw his shadow by the bathroom."

Heather was becoming unnerved as Travis ran around the side of the house where he saw foot impressions in the snow that stopped at the back door. Minutes passed with Heather pacing on the sidewalk, clinging to Harley, grateful for his Buzz blanket that shielded them both from the cool temperature. She knew Travis had gone inside the house through the back door. Suddenly, the front door opened, and he ran out, slamming it shut behind him. He looked at her and shrugged.

"I didn't see anyone."

"I forgot I have a gun in the nightstand," she whispered to him.

"Why didn't you get it?"

"I don't know . . . I panicked."

Heather saw that the other neighbors were coming out of their homes, and a small crowd was developing under the pine trees across the street. Heather looked past Travis and saw the shadow past her bedroom window. "He's still in there." Heather pointed frantically at the bedroom window as Travis turned and ran back up the steps and in the front door.

Heather attempted to give Harley to Evelyn, but he didn't want to be held by anyone other than her. So she placed him on the ground where he stood, refusing to let any of the neighbors touch him or his Buzz blanket.

Heather ran to the back of the house, just in case the intruder ran out the back door. She didn't know what she would do if he did, but at least she could tell the police which way he went.

The back door flung open, and to her dismay, the shadowy figure was running right at her. He obviously didn't know that there was no outlet in the back of the apartment.

The man ran past Heather just as the front door burst open, and Travis jumped down the steps and tackled him in the front yard.

"Get off me!" he yelled, jumping to his feet, pointing the gun at Travis. Without thinking, Travis lunged forward, grabbing the gun as a shot rang out into the air.

"Are you crazy?" He yelled throwing the man to the ground and snatching the .22 from his grip. "You could have killed someone, and breaking and entering would be the least of your worries."

The young man struggled to get up, but Travis's hold on him was unrelenting.

Heather walked over to scold the man for invading her home, but she stopped short when she saw that it wasn't a man but a teenager. As she got closer to the young man, he covered his face, and she could see his shoulders moving up and down.

"I'm sorry, Ms. Ford," he whispered, refusing to look in her direction.

Heather gasped loudly. "Jayden?" Tears filled her eyes. "Oh my God, Jayden, why would you do something like this?"

"I'm so sorry," he whispered as he wept in his hands.

Heather bent over and touched his face, which still resembled the young boy she had known four years ago. She couldn't take her eyes off him as he sat on the ground at her feet. He had so much promise, and she failed him. She wanted to take him in her arms and tell him everything was going to be okay, but she knew she was too late.

Travis saw hurt and disappointment etched in Heather's face as the police arrived and the lights from the cars bounced off the young man's face.

"What do you want to do?" Travis asked before going to meet the officers.

"I don't know." She shook her head in anguish, watching as the officer pulled Jayden from the ground and cuffed him.

"Sir, he's only seventeen. Please don't hurt him," she pleaded with the officer.

She wished they hadn't called the police because she didn't want him to go to jail.

As the officer placed Jayden in the back of the police car, Heather thought about his mother and the worry she must feel, not knowing where he is. Heather felt the need to have Harley close to her.

She walked across the street to where the crowd had gathered under the streetlight. The neighbors were standing, talking, and Harley was sitting on the ground under the tree. Heather walked over to him, smiling broadly, hoping to reassure him as he looked up at her. Their eyes met briefly, and in the darkness of night. She saw fear before he turned and looked at the ground. His tiny pouting lips turned up to let her know he was upset that she had left him.

You shouldn't have to explain these things to a three-year-old, she thought, reaching down and scooping him into her arms. He had the saddest look as he turned away from her, laying his head on her shoulder.

"I'm sorry," she whispered, kissing him on top of his head. His blanket shielded them from the chill in the night air. She stood in the dark shadow of the trees, hugging him tightly and allowing her tears to flow freely. She cried for Jayden. She vowed to do everything in her power to make sure Harley didn't fall victim to the streets. Realizing Harley had fallen asleep, she rubbed her nose against the back of his neck, knowing it was his tickle spot, but he didn't respond. Wiping away her tears with the back of her hands, she walked toward the house.

Travis was talking to the officer as Heather emerged from the shadow of the trees. He and the officer both watched as she crossed under the streetlight. His heart went to his throat when he saw her.

Heather looked first at the officer, then at Travis. The horror etched in their faces compelled her to look down. Both her hand and the Buzz blanket were covered in blood. She suddenly noticed the unusual weight of Harley's limp body in her arms, and as she touched the thick moisture against her cheeks, she knew.

She stopped walking and fell to her knees just as the officer and Travis pulled Harley from her arms. The officer laid the child's limp body on the ground and searched frantically for the wound. The blood now completely covered his face and hair.

Heather was on her knees, stroking her son's face gingerly while the officer performed CPR. She rubbed his hair that was now saturated with blood and felt her body go limp as her fingers touched the gaping hole behind his ear.

~

Silence.

Chapter Twenty

Ellis was on break when he got the call.

He was familiar with the street but not the address. He would never forget the street. It took him years to stay away from that side of town. Sometimes he rode down the main road, hoping to catch a glimpse of Heather at a light or gas station, but he never did. The fact that she never gave him a chance to explain himself left him with no sense of closure, and he carried a wound that never seemed to heal.

She hated him.

There was so much that he wanted to tell her.

He wanted her to know that he had filed for a divorce, but each time he called to tell her, she would answer the phone and tell him to respect her request—lose her number.

He hadn't spoken with her since he called to congratulate her when Harley was born.

He wanted to tell her that he loved her, and would never do anything to hurt her.

Somewhere in his heart he thought one day she would see him for who he was and give him a chance, but the thought of her having another man's child tore at his heart. When Mrs. Ford called and told him that she was pregnant he felt like he was losing her forever and decided to make a move and romance her.

But she found out about Lisa.

~

When he turned on the street, he realized the GPS was taking him right past her house. He slowed down to get by several police cars parked in the street and made his way through the crowds of people. His ride-along medic jumped out and ran through the crowd while he followed the direction of the officer so he could get close to the injured. He jumped out and hurriedly pulled the stretcher from the back. His adrenalin was building as he snatched his med bag and everything he would need to stabilize a gunshot wound. He saw several people crying as he made his way to where the officer had cleared a path. A woman standing in the crowd caught his attention, causing his heart to jump, but as he passed, he saw that it wasn't Heather.

He approached, and he was deeply saddened to see the paramedic working on what appeared to be a young child.

Dispatch didn't say anything about a young child, he thought as he placed the cot on the ground next to his partner.

"Stat?" There was so much blood he wasn't sure what he was looking at.

His partner didn't hide the tears in his eyes. "We got to move . . . gunshot wound to the head . . . keep applying pressure."

"I got him." Ellis reached down and carefully picked up the young child and turned to place him on the gurney. He wiped the blood from his face just as a woman who had been on the ground, praying, grabbed his arm. He turned, and there she was, standing right in front of him.

Seeing Heather was one thing, but the realization that the child in his arms was Harley was another.

"No. Heather, no!" Ellis moaned loudly and erupted in tears. "Tell me this is not happening."

~

He and Lisa married a month after they met, but after the first year she told him that she felt they had made a mistake. He tried everything to make her happy, but the harder he tried the more she seemed to resent him. He was certain she was having an affair and agreed that it would be best if they divorced.

At her suggestion, they continued living in the same house with Ellis spending most days and nights at the hospital. After a year the arrangement started to way him down. He had been working extra hours for month's trying to get the money needed to cover the cost of the divorce.

Whenever he crossed paths with Lisa she was always cold towards him until one morning when he stopped by the house to pick up a few extra clothes. Surprisingly, Lisa practically threw herself on him begging him for sex. He obliged, but couldn't help feeling the lack of love between them.

The night of Heather's accident, he was at the point where he didn't want to risk going home, and he was tired of the long hours at work. Heather being in the hospital gave him somewhere to go and someone to care about. Talking to Mrs. Ford and checking in on Heather every chance he got helped him begin the healing process, and the more he went to the hospital room, the easier it became to accept the end of his marriage.

He was becoming okay with the way things were until the day he came home and Lisa announced that she was pregnant.

In his heart, he knew the baby wasn't his. The unexpected pregnancy explained why she was all over him months earlier when he went by the house. She slept with him because she thought she was pregnant by someone else and was trying to cover it up.

He acted as if he was none the wiser, and although she had signed the divorce papers, they both agreed to wait until after the baby was born to file them. Lisa's morning sickness became increasingly worse as the months progressed and Ellis started spending more time at the house. The pregnancy became their alternative to reality, but he was not fooled.

The day Jacob was born, Ellis took one look at him and knew that he wasn't his, but since they were married, he decided there was no point in requesting a paternity test. He signed the birth certificate and soon after leaving the hospital dropped the divorce papers off with his attorney.

Surprisingly, he couldn't care less about Lisa's infidelities, but Heather's pregnancy felt like the ultimate betrayal. He didn't mind Lisa walking away because having Heather brought him comfort. Lisa being pregnant by another man didn't bother him because he saw Heather as the woman he wanted to bear his children. He thought that being a part of her life was laying the foundation for something bigger; he had no doubt in his mind that she would give him a chance.

He couldn't help thinking that Harley was supposed to be his.

He called Heather the day Lisa came home and told him about meeting her at the doctor's office. He felt relief knowing that he could finally tell her everything, but when she answered the phone she wouldn't let him get one word in; yelling and crying, she told him to stay away from her and her mother.

He never thought Heather would turn her back on him the way she did. When Mrs. Ford called him, he pleaded with her to allow him to explain everything before she passed judgment on him. She told him to come over so that they could sit down and talk.

He went to her house and poured his heart out to her. He told her that he was in love with Heather and wanted to be there for her through the pregnancy. In the end she told him that he needed to work on his marriage until it was over.

~

Ellis stared blankly at the wall in the waiting room, gently rocking Heather as he had done so many times years ago. Everything seemed to be playing in slow motion, like images in a dream. Two hours had passed since the paramedic pulled Harley's limp body from his arms as they rushed to get help. The anguished look in Heather's eyes cut deep into his heart as she pleaded with him to save her baby. He remembered the screams and knew they were his own as he cradled Harley, at the same time trying to keep him stable in the back of the ambulance.

He felt as if Harley was his son more so than Jacob. The lines were becoming blurred as his love for Harley deepened. Over the years, he and Harley had developed a bond that meant more to him than anything in the world. He never stopped calling Mrs. Ford, even after the news about his marriage broke, but he stopped visiting until after his divorce was finalized. After Harley was born, he stopped by several times a week to check on her and to play with Harley, whom she babysat while Heather was at work. Fresh tears pooled in his eyes as he thought about how happy Harley was to see him each time he walked through the door.

~

Heather wasn't aware of Ellis's presence, her mother praying silently, or anyone else for that matter. Her greatest fear was realized. For years she woke to the terrible dreams that were now her reality. Her body trembled with sadness, knowing that behind the brick wall, her baby was fighting for his life.

She prayed for hope and healing. She prayed for a miracle.

Cheri watched Ellis as he lingered around the family, playing on Heather's weakness to get close to her. Janet passed the time by tending to everyone's needs. They both knew that if Heather was not totally engulfed in the pain of the moment, she would've told him to leave a long time ago.

There was a collective sigh when the nurse appeared and reported that a major part of the surgery was over. She told them that they had removed the bullet and the doctor would be in shortly to speak with them. Mrs. Ford gasped loudly as tears erupted from her body. Cheri went over and comforted her as much as she could.

"I got her," Ellis whispered in Cheri's ear as Mrs. Ford fell in his arms and finally released tears she had been holding back all night.

"Ms. Ford, there is an officer waiting to speak with you," a nurse announced from the doorway.

Janet looked at the forlorn expression on her friend's face. "I'll tell them to come back?" she whispered.

Heather stood shakily. "No, I don't mind speaking with them."

~

The officer's heart went out to Heather as she entered the lobby. "Ms. Ford, Travis Horton provided us with most of what we need, but I have a few questions for you and I will need an official statement. How is you son?"

Heather felt a hand in the small of her back and was shocked to find Omar standing behind her. The look in his eyes and the pain etched all over his face spoke volumes. He was totally grief stricken.

"Heather, why didn't you call me?" Omar pleaded with tears in his eyes. "Where is he?"

Heather could smell alcohol as he walked past her and went to the nurse's station. "I need to know what's going on with my son." His loud voice broke the silence of the waiting room.

Heather's heart broke in several more pieces as she went to him.

~

For three years she ignored every attempt he made to be a part of Harley's life, and now with her son fighting for his life, she realized how wrong she had been. During her pregnancy, she received several text messages and voice recordings from him, trying to find out how she was doing. She made it a habit to delete all messages as soon as she heard his voice.

She and Cheri were out one evening when he called and left several messages requesting her delivery date. Cheri felt sorry for him and begged her to give him the courtesy of calling back, but she wouldn't. She was blinded by the pain of being burned by him and Ellis.

Everything collapsed around her when it was verified that the school didn't renew her contract. She went into survival mode. Trying to find a school that would hire her was the death of her. Interview after interview. And nothing.

The fact that she was single, pregnant, and would be out on maternity leave from November to January didn't help.

She didn't have time to entertain Omar with information about her pregnancy, and she didn't care about his feelings being hurt because she wouldn't return his calls. She was focused on one thing and that was making a life for herself and her baby. It was then that Cheri asked her for Omar's number so that she could communicate with him.

~

Taking his hands in hers, Heather spoke with a calmness that she didn't feel. "They removed the bullet, which was the hardest part of the surgery," she said, trying to reassure Omar. "We're waiting for the doctor to give us an update."

Omar grabbed Heather. "Heather, I'm sorry for treating you the way I did. I'm sorry. I was young and stupid. I know why you hate me, but please, let me see my son."

He was tired of being in the shadows.

"When Cheri called... I thought..." Tears filled his eyes. "He would never know how much I love him."

The last time he saw him was a couple of weeks ago on his birthday. Cheri sent a video of him opening his birthday gifts. Omar watched that video several times a day and smiled each time he watched Harley open the big Tonka truck he sent him. He also saw that Harley was his mirror image.

He remembered when he left the message on Heather's voice mail demanding a paternity test before she left the hospital. Cheri called him back, saying that Heather wanted her to let him know that no paternity test was needed because Harley wasn't his anyway. But Cheri reassured him by telling him that prior to him, it had been two years since Heather had been with anyone, and she hadn't been with anyone since him.

She was right because it didn't matter. Every month that passed, Harley was becoming more like him. That was something Heather couldn't deny.

Omar watched as Heather wiped the tears from her eyes.

"I'm sorry, I want you to know him. I hate that something like this had to happen for me to realize how selfish I've been."

She didn't know that Omar was there at the hospital, watching Harley from the window in the nursery when he was born. Cheri had called him when Heather started having contractions. When he got there, she and Janet made sure he got to hold Harley a brief moment before they returned the newborn to Heather.

Realizing the officer was standing patiently, waiting for her statement, Heather walked over with Omar's arms wrapped around her. "I'm ready to give my statement," she said with an inner strength that she hadn't felt in a long time.

The officer prepared his notepad. "Go ahead, ma'am."

"I want to start by saying that my son has made it through the hardest part of the surgery, and we're now waiting for the doctor to give us an update."

"Ms. Ford, I understand you are familiar with the suspect?"

"Yes, he was a student of mine some years ago. I brought him to my house on several occasions to help move some items to the school."

"So he had been inside your home before?"

"Yes."

"Do you know how he got into the house?"

"Yes. He entered through the back door. My son and I were inside, preparing for bed."

"Do you know where he obtained the firearm?"

"Yes. I keep a gun in my night table in my bedroom. It is registered."

"You are aware that he is facing charges that include breaking and entering and attempted murder and that, although he is seventeen, depending on the outcome of the surgery, we will be charging him as an adult."

"I know," Heather said sadly. "Officer, he is a good kid. He has suffered so much, and everybody, including me, turned their back on him."

"Forgive me if I don't share your sympathy, Ms. Ford, but we see this every day. Many of these kids were born in cultures that either prepare them for a life behind bars, or they don't see the age of twenty. These kids are born to die, one way or another." The officer shook his head sadly.

The officer turned to Omar. "This kid is no exception. In the last year we've picked him up for selling prescription drugs, vandalism, petty theft, now breaking and entering and attempted murder. We have to lock him up or the next call will be to the coroner."

Heather took Omar's hand and looked at the officer directly.

"I'm not sure about pressing charges," she said as her mind raced.

"What!" The officer and Omar looked at her in confused shock.

"Ms. Ford, I think you might want to consider what you're saying. This may not be the best time for you to—"

"I know what you're thinking." Heather whispered looking down at her trembling hands. "I just . . . remember working with Jayden. He had so much potential." Heather looked at Omar, almost pleading with him to understand. "I don't know what to do."

"Heather, he shot our son." Omar searched Heather's eyes, trying to see if she understood the magnitude of the crime. "Harley is fighting for his life. Do you realize that you are saying that you don't want this *delinquent* to receive punishment for this horrendous crime?" Omar paced the floor in total disbelief.

"I just feel like Harley's going to be okay," Heather said, trying to stop the horrifying images from playing in her head.

"But you don't know that, Heather, and you're making life-changing decisions without thinking." Omar couldn't believe they were arguing over this.

"Omar, listen to me. I don't believe in a life for a life. If I send that seventeen-year-old boy to jail, it's over for him, and I can't live with that thought. Before I sign his life away, I have to know that there is no blood on my hands. That I did everything I could to help him, and I can't say that. I know the system failed this kid because I was there."

The nurse announced that the doctor was ready to meet with the family.

Omar couldn't understand. "Heather, right now let's focus on Harley. Not this." He thanked the officer who left satisfied that they had a mutual understanding. When he took Heather's hand and turned to follow the nurse, dread consumed him.

Time stood still as they entered the waiting room. Janet and Cheri were so happy to see Omar walk through the door holding Heather's hand.

Omar's eyes never left the doctor's face. He wrapped his arms around Heather not for her support, but for his own. He was unaware of the overwhelming tension that his presence brought into the room as Mrs. Ford patted Ellis's knee reassuringly to keep him calm.

When the doctor saw that everyone was in the room, he advised the nurse to close the door.

He placed Harley's x-rays on the screen. "Due to the nature of baby Harley's terrible injury, this is a very delicate situation." His tone was low and deliberate. "The bullet entered behind the ear, near the mastoid bone, and stopped near the sixth cervical region of the spine. It was determined that the bullet had to be removed for the survival of the child."

"Our concerns with the removal of the bullet was that the space inside allowed no room for error. The bullet was lodged in front of the spinal cord which is an area that supports the neck. We were afraid of the amount of blood loss as well as what else we would find as the surgery progressed."

Everyone held their breaths as the doctor paused to look at the x-rays.

"The bullet has been successfully removed, and there doesn't appear to be any damage to the cervical or spinal cord, but I need you to be extremely patient with this process." He turned to Heather and Omar. "Harley has experienced a penetrating head injury that will require close monitoring over a long period of time. The bullet was still intact with no fragmentation, and we did not see any damage to the brain, but again it is very early in the process."

"Lord, I thank you," Mrs. Ford cried out as everyone joined in thanking God for the miracle that was taking place. Heather hugged Omar as tears clouded her vision.

"I can't tell you what the short- or long-term effects of his injury are at this time, but I can tell you that he is stable. The next twenty-four hours are going to be critical."

Heather's heart began to swell as she listened to the doctor. *God has granted me a few more days with my baby,* she thought refusing to let the situation, as horrible as it was, shake her faith. *The angels are walking Harley down the road of recovery back to me.* She looked at everyone standing around the room and thanked God that they were there. Omar stood by her side, and his presence gave her strength. She did not know what tomorrow would bring, but today, right now, she was able to exhale.

~

Heather followed the officer into the room and waited for Jayden to appear. She sat down in the chair, not sure how she felt about being inside the detention center. It had been two weeks since the break-in, and the officer told her that if she wanted to speak to Jayden she should come before he was moved. In the morning after his hearing he would be transferred to a permanent location to await his trial.

When the door opened and he stepped inside, Heather could see that his feet and hands were shackled. The officer bent over and released his feet to allow him to enter the room and sit down across from her. There was a glass separating them with a small hole in it, and she wondered if he would be able to hear her.

"How are you holding up?" she asked, watching his expression as he stared at the floor.

"I'm okay . . . I can't sleep though. Keep thinking about . . . what I did."

Heather could see the tears in his eyes as he spoke.

"I came to tell you that my son, Harley, is going to be okay."

Jayden looked up sharply. "I thought he—"

Heather didn't want him to say the words. "No, he's in the hospital. Very critical, but he's recovering."

"I am so sorry, Ms. Ford." He rested his head in cuffed hands and cried. "I don't know why I did it."

Sitting before her was a defenseless child struggling to survive in a world that had forgotten him just as the babies in her dreams. Heather wasn't sure if she was doing the best thing, but she knew what she had to do. "I'm not pressing charges." She said quickly. The words sounded strange even to her ears.

Jayden couldn't believe what he was hearing. No one had ever done anything for him. He looked at Heather, wondering why she was trying to help him after all that he had done.

"I know that the state has charges against you, but I will speak on your behalf if you do one thing for me."

"I will do anything you say, Ms. Ford."

"Give life a chance. The storms in our lives have brought us together for a reason. For four years God prepared me for this moment." Heather found an unexpected inner peace. "Jayden, God has a plan for your life." Tears filled her eyes as her dream was realized.

The Shadow

I know everything about you.
I have been with you since the day you were born.
I walk with you daily.
I dance as you dance.

I have never left you lonely,
But you look down on me because I am beneath your feet.
You walk on me, spit on me,
Never recognize me for what I am.

I know who lurks beside me.
I see him watching you,
Waiting for the moment to devour you.
But he is not I, and I am not him.

I know whose image you were crafted in, but me,
I was not worthy enough to receive a soul.
Look at me, I have no image.
I am left to lurk in the dark.

As we move in unison, I pretend that we are one and the same.
I know that my time with you will end when
you lie down for the last time.
I know that he will come for your soul and not your body.

That is the day you will leave me there in the grave.
I know that heaven has no place for me.
For I
Am only your shadow.

Edwards Brothers Malloy
Thorofare, NJ USA
March 2, 2015